Trooper Iron Eyes

Tracking down a wanted outlaw, Iron Eyes finds himself embroiled in the Indian wars. Badly wounded, he rides into Fort Liberty. Commanding officer Colonel Brice Jay assumes that the bounty hunter is near death, and takes a shine to his magnificent palomino stallion. When Iron Eyes recovers he finds that Jay has decided to take the stallion no matter what.

Deviously, Colonel Jay decides to send out a small party of troopers into the Indian-filled forest to rescue two abducted sisters from the hands of Sioux warrior Red Feather. Iron Eyes must lead the troopers or face execution for horse theft.

Trooper Iron Eyes

Rory Black

A Black Horse Western

ROBERT HALE

© Rory Black 2019
First published in Great Britain 2019

ISBN 978-0-7198-2963-5

The Crowood Press
The Stable Block
Crowood Lane
Ramsbury
Marlborough
Wiltshire SN8 2HR

www.bhwesterns.com

Robert Hale is an imprint
of The Crowood Press

To Chris Holt, a really nice guy

PROLOGUE

The surrounding forest and cleared ground suddenly fell eerily silent as the heavily painted warriors steered their ponies through the tall pines towards the solitary log cabin. It was as if every living creature within the confines of the dense forest knew what was about to happen.

The warriors were young, and yet experienced in what they intended doing. Time seemed almost to stand still as the braves slid from their bareback mounts and then proceeded on towards the cabin, smoke drifting from its stone-built chimney. As they slowly emerged from the dense undergrowth and studied the small cabin structure, the starlight danced across each of their determined features.

They were painted for action. Each of their faces and their glistening, exposed arms were decorated in the ritual adornment of each of the young braves' families. They wore their war paint with pride as once their fathers had done at an even bloodier time. For the Indians this was yet another time to prove their prowess as braves. They had all won their tribes' respect in similar raids on unsuspecting settlers as they vainly attempted to turn the tide of the constant flow of white intruders who had already changed their lands for evermore.

Like a well-drilled band of soldiers, they fanned out and took their positions around the small cabin. Their squinting eyes studied the wooden house and the few farm animals that were penned in makeshift corrals. Red Feather was the oldest son of the great Sioux chief Fire Mountain, and knelt holding his primed bow as he watched the house. This was the fifth time he had led his fellow braves in raiding the scattering of similar cabins that were dotted through the forested hills.

He had only one instruction, and that was to raze the cabin to the ground and kill anyone who attempted to stop them. White men were considered vermin by the numerous tribes covering the plains, and were to be destroyed. White females, however, were a different matter, especially those with fair hair. Every tribe knew how valuable any female was. Those whom they did not want as wives would be easily sold to lesser tribes for goods or horses.

Red Feather raised his head and then gave out a perfectly executed call that filled the clearing and echoed around the gathered warriors. To the innocent ears of most, it was just the cry of a bird in flight. To the more knowledgeable it was the call of an Indian instructing his fellow braves as to what they had to do next.

8

Hardly anyone outside the vast Indian territories knew of what was going on, and why things had deteriorated to this level in such a short period of time. There was little in the eastern newspapers of the true facts, and any reporting was heavily weighted in favour of the white men. Atrocities waged upon innocent Indians were never headlined.

It had not taken long for the various tribes to rebel against the constant infringement into their lands. Some settlers who had been tolerated for years were suddenly seen as the enemy by the enraged Indians.

The raging hostilities had swept across the vast plains in reply to the treaty violations. Practically every tribe in what were commonly called the Indian Territories had seen their legal ownership of their spiritual lands disregarded as the eastern government forged further and further west.

It seemed that it had become the unwritten policy to reclaim the lands by any means. If you escorted countless settlers and prospectors into the land which technically belonged to the native inhabitants and provided them with military protection, it was thought that the Indian problem would simply disappear. But the law makers who roamed the corridors of the marble Washington mansions did not know the men they were stepping upon: they totally underestimated the wrath and fury of the people they considered little more than savages.

War had already broken out in an area that spanned the total surface area of the whole of Europe. Yet for all the blood that was being spilled on both sides, little was ever reported in the newspapers back east.

Every day the death toll was growing. No one knew exactly how many Indians had fallen victim to the constant flow of settlers into their lands. The heavily armed cavalry had escorted most of them into the Territories, and did not keep records of how many of the people they called 'savages' were ultimately killed.

Various indigenous tribes who had been lifelong enemies were now joining forces in a vain attempt to stem the flood of white people who were claiming ownership of large chunks of the land under the protection of the cavalry.

Red Feather waved his arm at his fellow braves and watched as they closed in on the log cabin. As they did so he noted that the buckboard and its sturdy horse were not where Henry Smith usually kept them, close to the small structure. The skilled warrior realized that the elderly Smith must have driven his vehicle to the closest trading post ten miles away before the Indian and his warriors had arrived.

Yet the lantern light which spilled out from the log cabin made it clear that someone was inside, and Red Feather knew exactly who. He cupped a hand beside his cheek and warbled another perfect shrill: the two young females were alone inside the dwelling. A few equally perfected calls rang out across the clearing as the warriors returned his chilling call.

As the braves moved steadily towards the log cabin, none of them knew of the motives behind the continuous violation of their treaties. They had no idea that they were being deliberately provoked into fighting by a far superior force. Unbeknown to the Cheyenne, Sioux and numerous other tribes, the United States government had a plan which they thought would solve a multitude of problems. Washington politicians wanted the West settled, and all its native peoples removed by any means.

They had already placed a bounty on the heads of the buffalo that had once roamed the plains, and had practically made the animals extinct. This was a cunning plan aimed indirectly at the Indians, in that the destruction of the one animal the plains Indians relied on to feed and clothe themselves had been considered a far better option than actually fighting them.

However, the American government had totally underestimated the dogged determination of the proud native people. They would not simply roll over and die as had been assumed, but would fight by any means available.

But during the previous two years things had changed, as the number of troops in the heart of the Indian territory had been increased to record proportions. And the cavalry was spoiling for a fight – in fact the bloodier the better, for they had vast numbers of men fresh from the battlefields of the civil war. Some men relish the taste of blood, and once they develop an appetite for it, they can never satisfy their lust for more.

So it was with the majority of troopers who had been sent west after somehow surviving the bloody conflict that had pitched brother against brother. They had already tasted the blood of their enemy, and now were eager to add the blood of an utterly different type of foe, one which gave them an enemy of a different colour, an enemy they could kill without ever suffering the guilt that had dogged them since the war.

Henry Smith and his two daughters Loretta and Beth had known that the trouble was gathering pace, and even though they had heard that several of their fellow settlers had been attacked, they were unconcerned. For Smith had never had any problems with the local Indians since he had carved out the small clearing, and had even traded with them. That was why Smith had left his daughters unprotected in the cabin, and had travelled alone to the trading post for supplies.

From the cover of the trees the Indians moved closer to the small cabin. The shafts of lantern light cascading through the cracks of the door and windows caught the warriors as they moved from cover towards the cabin. Like bedazzled moths to an unguarded flame the warriors were drawn to the cabin. The closer the painted braves got, the more clearly they could hear the laughing females within the wooden structure. Loretta and Beth were blissfully unaware of the danger that was growing closer with every passing beat of their young hearts.

The starlight painted the area in a tranquil hue. There was no hint of what was to come. Only the wildlife in the dense forested surroundings remained silent, as though they instinctively knew what was about to happen.

Red Feather raced across the cleared ground and paused beside a three-foot tall tree stump. He stared with narrowed eyes at the window shutters. The sound of singing and laughter washed over the warrior as he pulled an arrow from a leather pouch which hung from his belt. He then carefully placed it on his bow string and signalled with a nod of his head to his followers.

The other braves raced from their hiding places and through the starlight. As Red Feather got to his feet he watched them crash against the door. Within seconds the braves had entered.

The singing abruptly changed to hysterical screams. Screams that echoed through the forest. Screams that it seemed nobody could hear.

ONE

Months passed, and the tension throughout the territory grew even tenser. At least eight farms had been attacked by marauding Indians since the raid on the Smith homestead, yet no one knew for sure how many of the Indian camps were also targeted. Yet for all of these atrocities, which had mainly gone unrecorded throughout the forests and plains, there seemed no hint of trouble as the gaunt horseman spurred his golden mount deeper and deeper into the uncharted forest.

The muscular palomino stallion moved between the trees with its unholy rider hunched over its neck upon the ornate Mexican saddle. The devilish bounty hunter studied the sun-baked ground as his horse carefully walked between the trees. Shafts of blazing sunlight cascaded down from the cloudless blue sky, but Iron Eyes kept his attention on the hoof tracks he had been trailing for more than a week.

He eased back on his long leathers and stopped the mighty palomino. He then looked up from beneath

14

the brim of his black sombrero. The hat had been plucked from the body of one of his last victims, Tequila Joe; the bounty hunter had decided that the outlaw no longer required a hat after he had placed two perfectly grouped bullets into Joe's chest. The shade from the wide hat brim prevented the merciless sun from burning the flesh off his skeletal face as he encouraged the large horse ever onwards.

Iron Eyes swung a long thin leg over the cantle of the saddle and dismounted. His eyes darted all around him as he lifted the closest flap of his saddle-bag satchel and pulled out a bottle of whiskey. The horse snorted, but its master ignored it as his sharp teeth pulled the cork from the bottle neck and then spat it on to the dusty ground. He finished the contents of the last third of the clear glass bottle and then tossed the empty vessel over his shoulder.

He ignored the sound of breaking glass as the bottle collided with a tree trunk and walked around the tail of the high-withered horse until he reached the other satchel. His long bony fingers lifted the leather flap and pulled out a bag of grain.

'If you weren't such a fast runner I'd not waste time and money feeding you, horse,' Iron Eyes said as he shook half the bag's contents on to the ground at the stallion's hoofs. 'Eat that, gluepot.'

As the palomino ate the oats, Iron Eyes returned the bag to the saddle-bag satchel. His senses were tingling and he did not like the unusual sensation. He rested an arm on the saddle and looked over its bowl into the surrounding trees. He tried to ignore the gut feelings that were tearing at him, but no matter how hard he tried, he still felt uneasy.

The forest had fallen silent hours earlier as he had entered the dense undergrowth and guided his mount through the maze of trees. But it wasn't the silence that troubled the painfully lean bounty hunter. Forests tended to fall eerily quiet whenever Iron Eyes entered them. He thought it was probably the aroma of death which hung on him that scared the critters and made them run for sanctuary – but this time it wasn't that.

It was something else.

Something which taunted his every fibre. He rubbed the palm of his hand over his horrific features and looked in every direction. The forest was filled with entangled undergrowth, which tended to keep spreading as the summer grew hotter. He knew that from painful experience.

He removed his hat and dropped it on the ground, and then pulled one of his canteens from the saddle horn and started to unscrew its stopper. The gaunt bounty hunter knelt and emptied half of the canteen's water into the upturned hat bowl. As he started to screw the stopper back into place his keen hearing detected the sound of movement to his right. As the palomino stallion drank from his hat, Iron Eyes ducked under the horse's neck and moved back to the saddle.

He glanced over the saddle in the direction of where he had heard the sound. As his long black hair fell over his cadaverous features he instinctively drew

16

one of his Navy Colts from his deep trail-coat pockets. His bony thumb pulled back on the weapon's hammer until it fully locked into position. The sound of the gun hammer locking filled the quiet woodland.

Iron Eyes narrowed his eyes as they searched for the maker of the noise that had alerted him. There was one thing for certain, he thought. He was not alone in this vast timberland.

The palomino raised its head and shook its cream-coloured mane as it finished its drink. The long legs of its master slowly moved from the saddle to the head of the mighty horse. As droplets of water dripped from the mouth of the stallion, Iron Eyes stooped, plucked up the sombrero and placed it on to his head.

The animal snorted as its painfully lean master continued to stare with unblinking eyes at the dense undergrowth. Iron Eyes patted the neck of the horse and then started to walk closer to where he had heard the mysterious noise. The stallion trailed him through the trees as though being led by an invisible tether.

Iron Eyes stopped and felt the nose of the palomino bump him in his wide back. He gritted his teeth and stretched his long frame up to its full height in a bid to see over the bushes before him. An entanglement of brambles and other forest greenery stood between Iron Eyes and whatever he had detected with his sharp hearing. But just as the bounty hunter was about to walk round the closest tree a chilling scream rang out. Iron Eyes swung on his boots as he caught a fleeting glimpse of an Indian flying through the undergrowth at him.

17

Before he had a chance to raise and aim his cocked weapon, the Indian crashed into him. As Iron Eyes fell backwards he could see that the painted warrior had a tomahawk in one hand and a knife in the other.

Both men hit the ground hard. Iron Eyes lashed out with his gun and knocked the knife from the hand of the frantic young brave. As the stunned bounty hunter managed to grapple with his muscular opponent he saw the tomahawk coming down towards him.

Iron Eyes swiftly moved to the right and the war club hit the ground where his head had been only seconds before. His bony hand grabbed the wrist of the young Indian and both men struggled for what felt like an eternity to the bounty hunter.

A dozen thoughts flashed through the mind of the gaunt Iron Eyes as he somehow held the Indian in check as they frantically wrestled across the dusty ground. Both men exchanged blows as they fought for their very lives and attempted to permanently end their opponent's existence. As blood flowed from their cuts and grazes, Iron Eyes wondered why the Indian brave had attacked him for seemingly no reason.

Then he remembered that for some inexplicable reason, Indians hated him. Practically every Indian, no matter what tribe they belonged to, detested the creature they all called the 'living dead man'. It seemed that they instinctively recognized Iron Eyes from the stories that were shared around their camp-fires.

The Indian raised his right leg and pushed it into

18

Iron Eyes' stomach, and lifted him off the ground. But even as the bounty hunter flew through the air he maintained his grip on the brave's wrists, and as he crashed to the ground he leapt back on to the young warrior, dragged his gun hand free and hit the brave across the jaw with his Navy Colt. The warrior's head was knocked backwards by the vicious impact of the blow. The sound of breaking teeth filled his ears as blood spewed from the Indian's mouth. The brave was stunned and helpless, but that did not stop the bounty hunter from finishing what he had already started. He drew his hand back, and then furiously battered the brave again with the body of his Navy Colt.

A sickening groan filled the surrounding area. With blood pouring from his mouth the young warrior swayed as another bone-breaking blow smashed into his face. His eyes rolled up and disappeared into his skull, and he went limp above the bounty hunter. Blood dripped from his cuts and splattered on to the gaunt figure. Iron Eyes mustered up every scrap of his sapped strength and threw the Indian aside, his eyes darting at his defeated foe.

'You sure are an ornery bastard,' Iron Eyes cursed. 'I'd have shot you but I got me a feeling you ain't alone in this damn forest. Something tells me that gunfire might bring a whole herd of screaming Injuns, and I'm too tuckered to fend off any more o' your kinfolk.'

Iron Eyes scrambled to his feet and stared down at the Indian on the ground beside him. He pocketed his Navy Colt and then kicked the Indian over until the warrior was on his back. His unseeing eyes stared up at the tree canopy as the bounty hunter walked around his unconscious body.

The bounty hunter glanced at the palomino stallion.

'That critter wanted to kill me, horse,' he growled as he nursed his bruises. He spat blood down on the painted young buck and then kicked the Indian again. 'I'm getting mighty tired of having to fight every damn Injun I meet up with. I'd have shot the bastard but there ain't no profit in it.'

The large horse snorted and pawed the ground. The action drew the attention of its master, and Iron Eyes looked at the palomino curiously. Without another word, he wiped the blood off his face with his coat sleeve and then plucked his hat back off the ground and placed it over his mane of long hair. He looked all around the seemingly desolate forest, but wasn't satisfied. Something in his inner self sensed that Indians were close. Too close for comfort. Just because his eyes couldn't detect anyone, it didn't mean they weren't there.

The horse had sensed something too, and the muscular palomino was rarely wrong. Iron Eyes watched the stallion's ears turn as they listened to sounds he couldn't hear.

'I reckon we'd best hightail it out of here, horse,' he muttered as he took up the reins and tossed them over the animal's wide shoulders. He moved to the alert animal's head and curled his bruised knuckles around its bridle. He pulled the palomino's head close to his own.

'What you heard, horse?' he asked the high-withered stallion as his eyes darted around the surrounding trees and undergrowth in search of whatever had spooked his handsome mount. The palomino took a step back, its eyes wide as it, too, searched for the origin of the sounds only it could hear.

'That's good enough for me,' Iron Eyes gripped the saddle horn and then threw his pitifully lean body on to the highly decorated Mexican saddle. His bony hands gathered up the reins as he poked both boots into the stirrups.

The powerful horse reared up as its emaciated master clung on and studied the undergrowth between the trees which surrounded them for s few seconds. Dust rose up as the stallion's hoofs hit the ground again.

'Let's get out of here, horse,' Iron Eyes whispered, as he turned the animal and then drove his blood-stained spurs into its flanks. But the palomino had barely reached a canter when the bounty hunter heard a familiar noise behind him. His bony hands gripped his reins even tighter. The sound of Indians whooping seemed to fill the forest around Iron Eyes and the handsome stallion. Iron Eyes stood in his stirrups as the horse gathered pace across the unstable ground. His head turned from side to side as the howls intensified.

Suddenly as if from nowhere, at least twenty warriors rose from the cover of the surrounding brush, their bows drawn and aimed at the bounty hunter. He dropped back on to his saddle and leaned over the neck of his mount, its creamy white mane flapping like the wings of a fleeing owl attempting to escape the talons of an eagle.

'Damn it all. This ain't good,' Iron Eyes growled as he frantically whipped the palomino's flanks with the ends of his long reins. The stallion increased its pace as another chilling crescendo filled the forest, its galloping hoofs eating up the ground as it sped between the tall straight pines. Iron Eyes realized exactly what he was hearing. He had heard the sound of arrows being fired from bows many times over the years.

Deadly projectiles came shooting through the air from all sides. They flashed all around him as he continually drove his spurs into the flanks of the golden stallion. Some missed their mark completely while others embedded themselves into the trees as Iron Eyes drove the horse between them.

The palomino leapt across a fallen tree trunk and crashed through a mass of entangled brambles. But as Iron Eyes steadied the horse a horrific sight suddenly faced him. He dragged the stallion back with all his might and stared in utter disbelief at another group of painted faces right in front of him.

Gripping the reins in his hands the bounty hunter's eyes widened in stunned surprise as he steadied the horse. It took every scrap of his riding skill to stay in the saddle as even more arrows flew past him.

Then the Indians primed their bows and released their venom at the startled bounty hunter. But as arrows rained in on him, Iron Eyes gripped the silver-topped saddle horn and dropped from his upright position to hang beside the stallion's rippling shoulder. He pulled one of his Navy Colts from his trail-coat pocket and cocked its hammer as the horse bolted forwards.

Like a powerful steam train in full flight the horse thundered at the Indians as Iron Eyes continually cocked and fired at the men before him. The cunning bounty hunter knew that the Indians would not willingly fire their arrows at the horse and risk hitting the magnificent stallion. Every arrow flew high over the saddle as the lean horseman clung like glue to the side of the charging palomino.

Bullet after bullet spewed from the barrel of the gun as the palomino stallion galloped straight at the line of warriors. One by one the braves fell to the ground. Then the huge horse ploughed straight through them.

Iron Eyes did not return to his silver-adorned saddle until he was certain the danger had passed. Then he hauled himself back upright and glanced over his shoulder as his mount continued to gallop between the countless trees.

After a mile or so, his scrawny hands drew back on the long reins and he slowed the powerful horse beneath him. When the palomino finally stopped, its hoofs sent a cloud of trail dust wafting between the trees.

He dismounted to check that his precious horse had not been hit by any of the arrows that had been directed at him, and then realized that his left hand was stiff. He flexed his fingers, and then noticed a trail of crimson running from his sleeve and covering his knuckles. He turned his head and stared at his shoulder.

An arrowhead was poking out just under his shoulder blade, and blood dripped off the sharp point of the flint tip. The shafts of sunlight filtering through the trees cast a gruesome shadow, and through narrowed eyes he could see the shape of the arrow's tail feathers on the ground.

Iron Eyes moved back to the saddle bags and fetched out another bottle of whiskey and pulled its cork with his sharp teeth. The smell of the hard liquor filled his flared nostrils as he placed the neck of the bottle to his lips. He drank half the bottle's amber contents and then gave a long, weary sigh. The encounter with the Indians had so excited him that he was only just noticing the pain of his wound. But he knew from experience that the pain would get stronger the longer he left the arrow in his emaciated body.

'Reckon I'd best dig this damn toothpick out of my shoulder before it starts hurting,' he told himself as he rested the bottle on top of a large boulder. He bent over and pulled the long Bowie knife from the neck of his mule-eared boot and stared at its sharp blade.

Then he placed a cigar between his lips and lit it with a match from his vest pocket. As he filled his lungs with smoke he knew that this was going to hurt. Pulling arrows out always hurt.

24

The gaunt figure moved to a tree and then backed up against its trunk. He pushed the arrow flight into its bark and moved swiftly. He heard the arrow snap and stared down at the blood-soaked feathers at his feet.

His bloody fingers picked up the whiskey bottle and carefully poured whiskey over the remainder of its shaft. He then stretched up his arm and dropped the cigar on to his whiskey-soaked back. The arrow and the back of his trail coat suddenly burst into flame.

The smell of the wood burning filled his nostrils as he placed the bottle back down, and his teeth gripped the cigar as he took a firm hold of the arrowhead. Then he pulled the arrow through his shoulder in one swift action.

His eyes filled with tears as agony charged through his tall, lean frame. Iron Eyes steadied himself as the burning liquor sizzled in his emaciated flesh. The stench of cauterized flesh filled his flared nostrils for a few moments as he staggered to the bottle. The scarred flesh around his hooded eyes focused on the bloody arrow in his grip as droplets of blood dripped from between his fingers. He tossed the arrow aside and then removed the cigar from his teeth and sat down on the boulder as his trembling hand picked up the bottle again.

He was shaking from head to toe.

Iron Eyes lifted the whiskey to his lips and took another long swallow. The burning of the hard liquor as it travelled down into his guts helped the slumped bounty hunter forget the unimaginable pain which tormented him. He got back to his feet and then strode up to the tall palomino and glared at the highly polished silver decoration which covered the saddle. His narrowed eyes looked at the reflection of the wound where he had just extracted the arrow. The wound had stopped bleeding and that satisfied the gaunt bounty hunter.

'That's the best I can do right now,' he muttered before looking back at the undergrowth he had forced the stallion through. His eyes tightened even more as he listened for any hint that the Indians had decided to continue hunting him.

He couldn't hear anything. The forest was silent again, but that did not convince the deadly Iron Eyes that he was free of the danger he had stumbled into a mile or so back. He ran his bloody fingers through his long black hair and then finished the contents of the whiskey.

He threw the empty bottle into the ferns, then reached up and grabbed the silver saddle horn. In one fluid movement the wounded bounty hunter put his foot into the stirrup and swung himself into his high saddle, and gathered up the reins. He turned the alert animal round and stared up into the tree canopies. The placement of the sun told him roughly where he was and what direction he would have to take if he wanted to escape the forest.

Slapping his long reins hard, Iron Eyes got the powerful palomino stallion moving again, and it made its way between the trees as its master continued to glance over his blood-stained shoulder. With every stride the intrepid horse took, Iron Eyes kept thinking about the fight he had somehow survived. He could not fathom why the Indians had attacked him, no matter how hard he tried. There seemed to be no particular reason for it, even though most of the natives scattered across the West always seemed to take a dislike to the ghostly figure that the bounty hunter had become. But this time something was definitely different, his mind kept telling him as the palomino continued to move its injured master ever onwards.

Iron Eyes glanced down at his bony hands. The crimson trails across one of his hands told him that he had started bleeding again. He gritted his teeth. He knew he had to find a safe place where he could tend his wound properly. He had to stem the flow of his precious blood before it all drained from his skinny frame.

He thrust his spurs into the flanks of his horse.

'Faster, horse,' he snarled. 'Quit dawdling.'

TWO

The mighty stallion had covered nearly five miles through the dense uncharted forest. The sun had set, and now a haunting moon sent eerie shafts of light through the densely growing tall straight trees. Yet Iron Eyes had not noticed anything as he kept urging on the large cream-coloured stallion with his bloody spurs.

The horseman knew that none of the far smaller ponies that most Indians tended to favour could have kept pace with the massive thoroughbred he sat astride. Finally he drew rein as he saw a crystal-clear, shallow river below him, the unnamed waterway carving its way through the dense growth of tall trees.

The stallion stopped as it sniffed the scent of the precious water it craved – though Iron Eyes did not intend allowing the horse to quench its thirst until he was sure it was safe. After five minutes the bounty hunter was satisfied there were no Indians anywhere within spitting distance. Slowly he released his firm grip and let the palomino descend the steep slope and emerge from the trees.

Moonlight flashed off the decoration that adorned the Mexican saddle as Iron Eyes summoned every last scrap of his dwindling strength to keep his mount in check. He knew the stallion might bolt and unseat him if he didn't kept it under firm control. As dust rose off the dry hillside and drifted into the cloudless heavens, the bounty hunter continued to glance all around as he leaned back against the silver cantle.

Both horse and rider could smell the welcome scent of water vapour as they neared the river. The waterway was less than three feet deep but moved at incredible speed across the rocks.

After what felt like an eternity to the horseman, the palomino eventually reached the flat ground. Iron Eyes let the horse walk into the river and start to quench its thirst. He slumped over the saddle horn as the stallion drank, and gritted his teeth. He had probably lost another precious pint of blood since he had pulled the vicious arrow out of his shoulder. His wound ached like the fiery flames of Hell itself – but that wouldn't stop the bounty hunter from getting out of this deadly forest.

He straightened up and let out a long breath.

The sound of the river as it continuously flowed over the rocky ground drowned out all other noises – but that made little difference to the determined bounty hunter.

For the first time in a decade he had been forced to quit hunting his chosen prey. The outlaw had left a clear set of tracks and Iron Eyes had followed them into the depths of the unholy forest, but even he could not continue his hunt.

His narrowed eyes glanced at his moonlit wound.

He doubted that the outlaw had fared any better and knew that it was only his experience with battling various tribes which had saved his own life. Most outlaws had none of his experience and knew nothing of the cunning of the Indians.

He reached into his pocket and pulled out a crumpled poster and shook it until he could read the solemn wording. 'Wanted dead or alive', and he sighed before dropping the poster into the fast-flowing water and watching it float away. 'Well, I figure nobody is gonna ever get a chance to claim that damn bounty money.'

He pulled an empty canteen off his saddle horn, unscrewed its stopper and then lowered it into the water by its long leather. The canteen quickly filled, and he retrieved it and his blood-stained hand returned the stopper. He hung the canteen next to his coiled saddle rope and then squinted hard at the forest across the river.

The eerie light of the moon cast a strange glow on the trees opposite, but Iron Eyes could just make out distant smoke as it trailed up into the sky.

'That must be the fort I've heard tell about,' he muttered to himself as his hands vainly searched for a cigar in his numerous trail-coat pockets. He could just make out one of the fort's high towers, but that was all. 'C'mon, horse.'

His bony hands pulled up the stallion's head out of

the cold water, then he tapped his spurs into its golden flanks and it started to canter through the river, sending plumes of water up from its hoofs. Within a few heartbeats the horse had reached the other side of the river and continued into the dense trees.

Iron Eyes spurred harder. He might have been badly wounded, but his only thought was that he was out of both whiskey and cigars. He drove his spurs hard into the freshly watered stallion and it started to eat up the ground beneath its hoofs.

The rider hung on for dear life itself as the palomino thundered through the seemingly endless trees. The bounty hunter had been riding for more than an hour when his flared nostrils filled with the unpleasant scent of civilization. He could smell chimney smoke and the putrid stench of outhouses in sorrowful need of lime. It was a combination that always told the weary traveller when he was close to finding fellow human beings.

Iron Eyes could see droplets of blood floating in the air as he hung desperately on to the mane of the powerful stallion as it continued to obey his spurs.

The gaunt bounty hunter knew only too well that he had to find somewhere to tend his bleeding wound before his pounding heart pumped every last drop of blood from his malnourished body. Time was running out.

He recalled the tops of the wooden structure he had observed earlier. Every sinew in his pain-racked form told him that he had to reach there while there was still time to tend his wound.

Like a man possessed by a herd of demons, Iron Eyes started to whip the shoulders of the large horse, even though every movement of his arm was a torture.

The haunting moonlight glanced across the muscular horse as it carried its blood-drenched cargo further and further away from the deadly natives.

The palomino stallion obeyed its weakening master and crashed through undergrowth like a racing locomotive. The magnificent stallion was practically guiding itself through the rough terrain now as Iron Eyes slumped in his saddle and simply gripped the silver saddle horn and gritted his teeth.

The huge horse thundered on through the trees as the delirious bounty hunter caught the scent of men and horses ahead of him. His narrowed eyes opened and he tried to focus. He knew the scent of both Indians and white men alike, and although he did not care for either breed of creature he felt a sudden wave of relief in the knowledge that he was closing in on an encampment manned by folks who would not fire arrows at him. Though white folks did tend to fire their guns at him.

THREE

A mile of trees had been cleared around the large fortress and used to construct its buildings and its walls. Fort Liberty was a massive military outpost by any standards, and had achieved its purpose in sending a stark warning out to the numerous tribes who once roamed these lands unchallenged. It stood on the very edge of the vast Indian territory and covered more than twenty acres. Hastily constructed due to the growing attacks upon the settlers in the region by Lakota braves from various Sioux tribes, the fort boasted the tallest walls and the largest number of cavalry within a hundred miles.

The government back on the eastern seaboard had gradually realized that the vast land they had legally gifted to the various tribes was far more valuable than they had originally thought. The lumber alone was worth a fortune, and the recent discovery of gold had only added to its value.

It seemed to the American government that they would have to get the land back without actually seeming to steal it. At first they had placed a bounty on the heads of the nomadic herds of buffalo, and millions of the animals had been slaughtered. It was common knowledge that all the plains Indians relied upon the passing of the buffalo as they migrated on their regular route, and if you could eliminate them, the Indians would soon follow.

Starvation was meant to eliminate the problem of the Indians, but the eastern government had not understood that men of any colour do not just roll over and die.

They fight.

That was why they had constructed so many similar forts across the land which in actual fact did not belong to them. Yet when the Indians started to object and rebel against the ever-increasing number of settlers and prospectors being escorted into their land by thousands of troopers, they only played into the hands of the men back in Washington.

Indians were being portrayed as savages, when in reality they were only trying to protect what belonged to them. The Indians who had initially been peaceful towards the white intruders had suddenly started to fight back.

Newspapers across the land proclaimed that the Indians were bloodthirsty monsters who would massacre every single person they encountered. Having no voice of their own in the palaces of power, they could do nothing but fight.

Fort Liberty had more than a thousand troopers and even more horses. The buildings inside the walls of the fort contained everything an enlisted man might require, with the exception of female company. More than ten large structures encircled the enormous parade ground, from bunkhouses for the soldiers, well-equipped stables, to a section for the married officers.

Directly opposite the large wooden gates, beneath a hand-carved façade bearing the fort's name, stood the main building where the officers worked.

A twenty-foot square trading post which bought and sold the mundane items required by the military stood close to one of the four sentry towers, and did a roaring trade. The outpost welcomed most of the drifters who occasionally visited Fort Liberty to replenish their provisions. Most, but not all.

As the gallant palomino cleared the trees and started to race across the distance between itself and the massive fort, its barely conscious rider had no idea of the reception he was about to receive.

Sentries moved along their high parapets to the towers on each side of the massive gates that guarded the entrance from intruders, and aimed their rifles at the handsome horse and its slumped rider. Under the light of the large moon the horseman looked even more horrific than usual. One of the troopers glanced over his shoulder and shouted down into the courtyard:

'Rider approaching!'

Within seconds Captain George Baker had mounted the wooden steps to the parapet and moved swiftly to the shoulder of the trooper who stood beside three of his fellow sentries.

Baker squinted into the ghostly moonlight.

'Who the hell is that?' he questioned.

'I don't know,' Jody Casson replied as his finger stroked the trigger of his rifle. 'But whoever he is, he's riding one mighty good-looking horse.'

'What's a Mexican doing this far north, sir?' one of the troopers asked the thoughtful officer as he, too, brooded on the strange sight before them.

'That's a good question, trooper,' Baker sighed. 'I sure wish I knew.'

'It might be an Injun,' Casson remarked as he licked his thumb and ran it across his rifle sights. 'Maybe I oughta shoot the varmint.'

Shaking his head, Baker rested his arms on the pointed tops of the wall and tried to identify the rider. He mopped his brow and then removed his hat and shook beads of sweat from it before placing it back on his slicked down hair.

'Who is that on that palomino?' he asked aloud. 'All I can see is blood staining his trail coat. By the looks of it he's tangled with some of our feathered friends out there.'

'It might be a trick to get us to open the gates, sir,' one of the soldiers stated. 'He might kill a fair number of us once he's inside the fort.'

'I surely doubt it, son,' Baker said. 'By the looks of that rider, he's closer to our Maker than any of us want to be.'

Trooper Casson shrugged. 'I'm keeping my rifle aimed on him just in case.'

'Good thinking, trooper,' Baker patted the soldier on his back and then walked along the parapet. He stared down into the huge parade ground.

As the mighty stallion drew closer to the fort, Baker moved away from the wall and shouted down at two troopers standing beside the gates.

'Open up the gates, men,' he ordered. 'We've got a badly wounded man headed here.'

The troopers lifted the hefty wooden barricade and then pulled one of the gates wide open. As the troopers stared out into the moonlight Captain Baker quickly descended the steps and watched the muscular palomino approach.

The officer lifted the black leather flap of his holster and pulled out his service pistol. Baker cocked the gun's hammer and stood beside the troopers next to the gate.

All three men watched the handsome horse moving towards them with its half-conscious rider slumped on its neck. Baker felt the hairs on the nape of his neck tingle as his inquisitive eyes stared at the motionless figure.

'That's a redskin, sir,' one of the troopers said as he drew up his rifle and trained it on the approaching palomino. 'Look at his hair. It's a trick.'

Baker stepped between the concerned trooper and the magnificent stallion. He too had noticed the mane of long black hair as it bounced on the rider's back – yet something told him that this was no Indian.

'Don't fire,' Baker ordered.

The stallion had slowed its pace and came to a standstill just inside the parade ground. As the troopers closed the gates and secured them again, Captain Baker moved to the neck of the snorting horse. He still had his six-shooter aimed at Iron Eyes as he studied the horseman carefully.

Baker waved to the troopers on the high parapet and signalled them to come down on to the parade ground. The three men ran down the moonlit steps and across the sandy ground to the officer.

'Get this man off the back of this horse, men,' Baker instructed the three troopers. 'Take him to the infirmary and get the doc to check him over.'

'Ain't he dead?' asked the trooper closest to the blood-soaked bounty hunter. 'He sure looks dead.'

The other troopers stared down at the motionless figure of Iron Eyes as they lowered him to the moonlit ground. Each and every one of them agreed with Jody Casson, the bounty hunter looked more dead than alive.

'Pick him up and carry him to the doc's,' Baker ordered again. He stood silently as the men obeyed his orders and picked up the limp Iron Eyes and balanced his scrawny body between them.

'I still reckon he looks dead, Captain,' Casson groaned as he wrapped his arm around the bounty hunter's left leg. 'We'd be better off carrying this poor critter to the morgue.'

Although Baker was in silent agreement with the enlisted men that Iron Eyes did appear dead, something deep down told him that a spark of life still burned in this strange-looking creature. He waved his hand at the troopers, and watched as they shuffled across the sandy ground towards the doctor's quarters. The lean officer then swung round on his boot heels and climbed back up the wooden steps to the parapet. After reaching the high wall, Baker holstered his pistol and stared out at the forest that surrounded Fort Liberty.

'I reckon the doc is the best qualified man to decide that, trooper,' he muttered, resting his hands on the pointed wooden logs of the wall. Then he sighed, and whispered under his breath: 'Something just tells me that pitiful critter ain't dead.'

FOUR

The commanding officer of Fort Liberty was a man with more than twenty years' active service in the cavalry. Colonel Brice Jay had been a seasoned officer long before the civil war had added even more medals to his collection, and he had risen up through the ranks at an uncommon pace. Jay had been considering his future long and hard before he was appointed the first man to command the massive fortress. But multiple injuries had prevented him from leading his men into battle in the latter part of the war, and he had been forced to take a desk job in Washington.

Unlike many of his contemporaries, however, Jay did not have contacts in the marble halls of power. He had wondered about entering politics where the rewards were far greater than anything a regular soldier could earn, but many of his military rivals appeared determined to keep him out. Thus it seemed that Brice Jay was doomed to end his days sitting at a desk until his meagre pension was finally due. He had been a widower for five years, and was weary. Since the end of the war, life had become difficult for men of his age and rank: it was as though their existence was of no further use.

Jay was known for his courage in battle, but for a short while there had been no battles. Then out of the blue he received instructions to head west to where a new war was brewing. He was to be the commanding officer of a newly constructed fort set on the very edge of the infamous Indian lands. The Indian wars had grown out of all proportion, and the government wanted a tried and tested officer to wipe out all the hostile natives and to assist in the migrating settlers.

Although he did not relish the responsibility of becoming an officer in this furthermost cavalry outpost, Jay hated the job he had been forced to accept in Washington. He had never been west of the Pecos river, and his only knowledge of Indians had been gained from reading dime novels and newspapers, which were full of exaggerated stories designed to feed the insatiable appetite of the Easterners. Furthermore his only knowledge of the Indian troubles was that for some reason, the natives had become rebellious.

To men cut from the same cloth as Jay, it had not seemed too difficult a task. But he had spent six months in Fort Liberty, and every moment had felt like a lifetime. He simply could not understand what was going on, and why the Indians had started to attack and kill when they had been peaceful for years.

Brice Jay had been a valiant soldier for two decades and knew nothing of the government's motives. To him, everything was black and white, there were no grey hues. He was naïve and unable to read between the lines. He had lived his entire life by the rule book, but now he was starting to suspect that his superiors back east had an ulterior agenda. He was becoming convinced that the Indians were simply responding to some dire injustice that he was not aware of.

Over the years Jay had never questioned anything his superiors told him, like all good soldiers tend to do. He had obeyed his orders blindly. But now his daily routine was filled with nagging doubts, and these tormented the seasoned officer. Every sinew of his body wanted to confront the powers back east, but like all men of his advancing years, he feared losing his pension and being branded as a troublemaker. Jay had always been patriotic – but now he was also curious. But it was a conflict contained inside his own soul, and one that he could not share.

His tired eyes looked up from the mass of papers he was meant to be reading and focused on the wall clock. It was far earlier than the darkness outside the log construction indicated. He opened a large silver cigar box and drew out one of the expensive Havanas. After cutting off its tip he placed it between his teeth and then struck a match across his highly polished boot. The smoke tasted good to the colonel.

A slight tapping on the office door was followed by a well-built man who quickly entered and strode to the desk. Sgt Leo Tolley looked through the cigar smoke at the tired officer.

'Henry Smith is outside again, Colonel,' he said.

Jay savoured the flavoursome cigar and did not answer until he had exhaled. He glanced at Tolley.

'Why does that man bother me all the time?' he moaned. 'I'd help him if I could, but it's just too risky. I can't risk the lives of a troop of our enlisted men looking for his daughters.'

Tolley nodded in agreement. 'You're right, Sir. Smith's daughters could be anywhere by now. Them forests are bursting with our red brothers and every single one of them would happily kill anyone who entered. Soldiers would be top of their scalping list.'

Even though Brice Jay knew the danger of sending men into the increasingly hostile forest, something was gnawing on his conscience. He wanted to help Henry Smith if only he could find a way of doing so.

'I reckon you're right, Leo,' Jay said as he stared through the cloud of smoke which hung over his desk. 'The trouble is I just hate not trying. Men like Smith are helping to settle this country and they deserve all the help that the cavalry can provide.'

Tolley had been constantly at the colonel's side for three years and knew the weary man better than most. He had witnessed many men like Jay over the years, men who were unable to adjust to the stark differences between the brutal civil war, state against state and their bloody battlefields, and this strange conflict. The Indian wars were totally alien to men who lived by the rule book. The Indians fought instinctively, and knew nothing of Jay's type of battles. There were no gentleman's rules: they fought to win and then fled, and after a while returned to fight again.

Every single fact that had served Jay well over the years meant nothing out here. This was an entirely new type of war, and one which did not respect any of the things that Brice Jay held dear. This troubled the veteran colonel as he stared through the lamplight at the open office door.

Tolley poured out a tall glass of brandy for his superior and placed it in the ink blotter.

'Drink that, Colonel,' he sighed, as he glanced over his shoulder to his own office. He looked back to Jay and then rested his hip on the carved wooden desk border. 'Smith has been sitting out there for three hours. I feel sorry for that man.'

'Sympathy is something I don't approve of, Leo,' Jay said sternly as he lifted the glass to his lips and took a mouthful of brandy. 'Smith needs help. I wish I could help, but for the life of me, I just can't think of an answer to this problem.'

'You will, Colonel,' Tolley said. 'You always do.'

As Jay lowered the glass from his lips he stared hard at the sergeant and raised his eyebrows.

'I'd like to have your faith, Leo,' he said, 'but it's just not justifiable to send out enlisted men on such a suicidal mission, and you know it.'

Tolley shrugged. 'You'll figure out a way we can help Smith, Colonel.'

Jay pressed his fingertips together thoughtfully.

'This is a troublesome case,' he sighed. 'Refresh my memory of its details, Leo.'

Tolley nodded and looked at the ceiling before speaking.

'Before we arrived here at Fort Liberty, Smith had both his daughters kidnapped from his cabin,' Tolley began. 'He's been practically begging the cavalry to send a platoon of troopers into the forest to try and rescue them gals ever since.'

Brice Jay sucked hard on his cigar and then wallowed in its smoke. He bit his lip and shuffled the unread papers on his desk as his mind tried to think of a course of action. Finally, he looked straight at the sergeant.

'This is a suicide mission to anyone who attempts it, Leo,' he muttered. 'Only a small band of men have the slimmest of chances of managing to get in and out of that forest alive. It would also require the services of a scout who can think like an Indian to guide them. How could I justify sending any of our boys out there?'

Tolley shook his head slowly.

'Smith told me that he is willing to go on this mission himself, Colonel,' he remarked as he looked out of the corner of his eye at the seated Jay. 'And suicide mission or not, I'm willing to tag along too and look for them gals of his.'

It was as though the sergeant's words had ignited a devilish idea in the seasoned officer's brain. Brice Jay suddenly glanced at his sergeant with admiration etched in his rugged features as he exhaled a cloud of smoke at his right-hand man. He tilted his head and smiled at Tolley.

'Damn it, Leo,' he said before standing. 'I've just had an idea that might work.'

'You have?' the sergeant nodded.

45

'I sure have,' Jay nodded enthusiastically before clapping his hands together and pointing at his underling. A wry smile covered his normally impassive features. 'Round up all the troopers in the stockade and bring them in to see me, Leo.'

Tolley raised an eyebrow.

'But why?' he questioned.

'You'll find out soon enough,' Jay filled his lungs with the smoke of his cigar and watched as Tolley turned on his heels and headed for the door. 'Apologize to Smith on my behalf and tell him to be here at nine in the morning.'

The sergeant paused.

'I got me a notion I know what you've got planned!' He smiled before leaving the office.

Jay finished his brandy and pushed the empty glass back towards the decanter and refilled it with the amber liquor. He felt confident that he might have the solution to Henry Smith's dire problem.

Jay knew that it was a tough call. Locating the two girls in such a dense landscape might seem virtually impossible – yet the colonel was a man who believed in miracles. He had faced certain death many times and somehow survived. He downed the strong brandy and rested the glass on his ink blotter.

All he needed was a miracle.

He moved to the small window and stared out on to the moonlit parade ground. He was about to return to his desk and await the arrival of his trusty sergeant and the stockade prisoners when he spotted the large palomino stallion standing close to the gates. The

46

colonel knew of no one who owned such a powerful horse in or around Fort Liberty.

With a growing curiosity, he grabbed his hat off the stand and placed it over his silver hair, and marched out of his office. Within seconds he was halfway across the parade ground heading to where the sturdy stallion stood.

FIVE

The army post was still bathed in a blanket of eerie moonlight as the three troopers carried the motionless body of the infamous bounty hunter into the doctor's quarters. The nervous figure of acting medical surgeon Samuel Duffy struck a match and put its shaking flame to the wicks of the two lamps. As he lowered the glass funnels down and adjusted the brass wheels so the interior of the office was filled with the warm artificial light, he stared at the body the three troopers had rested on the long wooden table before him.

'Who the hell is this?' Duffy asked the enlisted men.

Only Jody Casson spoke.

'Captain Baker told us to bring this pitiful critter here, Sir,' he said dryly. 'Damned if I know why. I ain't no expert, but he sure looks dead to me.'

Duffy brushed the long black hair off the face and then reeled back in shock as he saw the hideously scarred face which had been previously hidden from view.

'Oh my God!' he exclaimed as he forced himself to focus on the brutalized face of Iron Eyes. 'This critter don't even look human.'

Casson nodded in agreement as his fellow troopers left the confines of the doctor's workplace. He edged closer to the shoulder of the stunned officer and shook his head.

'I ain't ever seen anyone that looks like this pitiful bastard,' he muttered. 'Look at his face, Doc, look at his face.'

'I'm trying not to, trooper,' Duffy sighed as his hands peeled back the blood-stained clothing to expose the wound where Iron Eyes had torn the arrow from his flesh. Blood was still weeping from the savage wound. Duffy leaned over and studied it more carefully.

'Was he shot?' Casson asked.

'Nope,' Duffy replied as he probed the crimson mess. 'This ain't a bullet hole. It's the hole left from an arrow shaft.'

'You mean that he pulled the arrow out?' Duffy gasped.

'Yep, that's what he did,' Duffy answered after inspecting the blood-stained hands and carefully turning Iron Eyes over to expose the burnt fabric of his trail coat. 'He must have set fire to the arrow after somehow breaking off the arrowhead. This scrawny critter then pulled the wooden shaft of the deadly projectile out of his chest. Look, you can still see splinters in the wound.'

Casson sniffed the air. 'Is that whiskey I smell?'

Doc Duffy nodded. 'Whoever this man was, he was well practised in tending his own wounds. By the looks of him, he'd done this many times before. I'm just surprised that he managed to live as long as he did.'

'How come he died, Doc?' the trooper wondered.

The expression on the face of Duffy went grim as he looked down upon what he imagined was a dead man. He glanced at the enlisted man and raised his eyebrows.

'By the state of his clothing I'd say that he bled to death, Casson,' he sighed. 'I'm just sad that he reached the fort too late for me to help him.'

Suddenly Duffy felt a shock race through him as the wrist of his left hand was grabbed by Iron Eyes' bony fingers. Both men took a backward step but only Casson managed to put distance between himself and the apparent body.

Doc Duffy felt the skeletal fingers gripping his flesh with unimaginable strength. Slowly his eyes looked down on the bounty hunter. To his surprise Iron Eyes was glaring back up at him.

'You're alive,' he stammered as the soldier looked on in awe.

'I don't die easy,' Iron Eyes whispered before releasing his grip on the startled doctor.

Cautiously the speechless trooper returned to the side of the shaking medical officer and rubbed the sweat off his face with his shirt sleeve.

'He's alive, Doc,' Casson managed to say.

As Duffy massaged his wrist he nodded in agreement.

'I don't know how, but he's alive OK,' he croaked.

Iron Eyes gritted his teeth and glanced at his bleeding wound and then returned his piercing stare at what his dazed mind had already worked out was a doctor.

'Sew this damn wound up,' he snarled through his scared lips. 'Stop the bleeding so I can get out of here.'

Duffy nodded and pointed to an enamel bowl filled with the tools of his trade. As his fingers hastily threaded catgut through a large needle he watched the hideous face turn to look at the startled trooper. Jody Casson felt as though he were looking at the Devil himself as he vainly tried to swallow. There seemed to be no life in the bullet-coloured eyes that studied him.

'Quit looking at me,' Casson croaked.

The bounty hunter raised an arm until his long bony fingers found a bloodstained pocket and fished around in its damp material.

The eyes of the trooper widened as he watched the long skeletal fingers pull out a ten-dollar bill blotched with scarlet gore. Iron Eyes handed the bill to the trooper.

'Go get me a bottle of whiskey and as many cigars that this will buy, soldier boy,' the bounty hunter growled.

'Should I, Doc?' Casson asked the doctor.

Then the room filled with the sound of a Navy Colt being cocked as Iron Eyes managed to pull one of his infamous guns from his deep trail coat pocket. Iron

Eyes waved the primed weapon between the two startled men.

'If you don't,' Iron Eyes warned. 'I'll surely kill you.'

Duffy nodded at Casson.

'Get him the whiskey and cigars, trooper,' he said
before leaning over his patient with his needle in his
still shaking hand. 'And be quick about it.'

SIX

Colonel Brice Jay had remained silent since reaching the high-withered palomino stallion. He had studied the magnificent animal carefully, and desired the creature more than any other horse he had seen since the end of the war. It reminded him of his own valiant steed which had fallen during the last great battle of the civil war. His imagination could almost see the powerful stallion in its finest livery. There was no mistaking the quality of the stallion.

'You would make a fine charger,' Jay muttered under his breath as he continued to inspect the palomino. 'What on earth are you doing out here in this godforsaken land?'

The moonlight masked the cuts and grazes that were evidence of the tough encounter the palomino had managed to survive. The ornate Mexican saddle only added to the curiosity which burned inside the commanding officer as he walked around the animal and admired every inch of the powerful beast.

'Good-looking animal,' a voice drew his attention

briefly from the stallion.

Jay turned and watched the far younger George Baker as he approached from the wooden steps of the fortress wall. The colonel turned to face the captain and nodded.

'Indeed, Captain,' he said. 'Was its rider a Mexican?'

The captain shook his head. 'He didn't look anything like a Mexican, Sir.'

'Strange.' Jay sighed rubbing his whiskered jawline.

Baker slowed his approach as he reached his superior officer and patted the muscular stallion. He then rested his knuckles on his belt and looked at his superior from beneath the brim of his hat.

'It sure is,' he agreed. 'I think its dishevelled rider owes his scalp to this handsome mount.'

The colonel looked at the younger officer.

'Where did this magnificent horse come from, Baker?' Brice Jay wondered as he noticed the moonlit blood that stained the side of the palomino. Upon closer inspection he reasoned that it must belong to the animal's master.

Baker narrowed his eyes.

'About thirty minutes back the sentries spotted a rider burst out from the forest,' Baker began to relate. 'The rider was just slumped over the neck of this horse. As it approached, we opened the gates and this big fella brought its master into the parade ground.'

Jay shook his head in silent admiration for the sturdy horse beside them. His thoughts then drifted to the man who had been riding the astounding stallion.

'By the looks of it, the poor man was in a bad way,' Jay indicated with a glance at the bloodstains on the stallion.

'More dead than alive,' Baker agreed.

Brice Jay looked from under the brim of his hat at the captain and frowned. 'Are you telling me that this horse's master was still alive after losing this much blood?'

George Baker had little experience of wounded men as he was fresh out of military school. All he could do was go by his gut instincts.

'I think so, sir,' Baker nodded. 'I had a few of the troopers carry him to the doctor's quarters, but as you say, that horseman had spilled a lot of blood and it's doubtful that he survived his wounds.'

The captain's words had only seemed to increase Jay's interest in the stallion. As the commanding officer of Fort Liberty it was well within his rights to take possession of anything he desired. And he desired the palomino more than anything else he had seen since travelling west.

The colonel paced around the stallion again, all the while studying it – and the more he observed the palomino, the more he wanted it for himself. He tried to look unimpressed by the animal, but even the eerie moonlight could not conceal the growing smile that crept over his face. He paused by the noble head of the muscular mount and fired an order at Baker:'Take this stallion to the stables, Captain, and have it watered, fed and cleaned up.' He said with a dismissive wave of his hand: 'Put it in my private stall and tell the blacksmith to spare no expense. I want that horse brought back to its best in quick-time.'

'Understood Colonel,' Baker saluted, took the palomino's reins and led it towards the vast livery stables.

Jay was about to return to the officers' quarters when he noticed the trooper running from the supply store back towards the doctor's quarters. At first the colonel was going to ignore the sight of one of his enlisted men moving hurriedly through the numerous shadows which carved strange patterns across the sandy parade ground, but then he recalled that Baker had told him that the magnificent palomino's master had been taken to the doctor's for treatment.

'Now why is that trooper running so quickly?' he asked himself. It might have ended at that, were it not for a nagging desire to discover the fate of the stallion's owner. If he were dead that would simplify things, Jay reasoned.

Jay had never been a man to suffer from avarice before, but after setting his eyes on the stallion, a strange desire had swept over the highly decorated officer, and he wanted that horse more than anything he had encountered in this unholy land. Every sinew in his frame knew that it was wrong, but he actually wanted the owner of the palomino stallion to succumb to his injuries. After all, Jay told himself, he did not know the horseman personally, and if he were dead it would be as meaningless to him as was the sight of the thousands of dead soldiers on the many battlefields he had experienced during the war. Death meant nothing to the embittered soldier.

Without even realizing it, Jay was walking toward the medical quarters. He crossed the parade ground and looked up at the dozen or more sentries who walked the parapets with their rifles clutched in their hands. Then his attention was drawn to what lay straight ahead of him: a door was slightly ajar, and lamplight cascaded from the interior of the building and reached out across the sandy ground. He marched, like all old soldiers would be wont to do, towards the source of the light.

Colonel Jay stepped up on to the boardwalk outside the sizeable structure and paused for a moment as he removed his hat and flattened down his white hair neatly. His mind raced as he stood beneath the porch overhang and listened to the loud voices coming from within the building. He was puzzled by the noise, as he had not expected anything but respectful silence. He pushed the door further open and entered.

It took a few moments for his eyes to adjust to the brightly illuminated room. He then noticed Doc Duffy bent over the patient as the trooper opened the box of cigars next to Duffy's shoulder. Jay cleared his throat and made his way closer. Duffy glanced up and acknowledged the officer.

'Howdy, Colonel,' he said.

Brice Jay was confused by the sight, which was not what he was expecting. He placed his hat down on a cabinet and moved to the edge of the long table and

57

stared down at Iron Eyes.

The bounty hunter had a cigar between his razor sharp teeth and was propped up as the doctor feverishly sewed up the hole in his scrawny frame.

'I was led to believe that this man was nearly dead, Duffy,' Jay muttered as he surveyed the tall, unwashed specimen before him. 'Captain Baker said that he doubted there was anything that could be done for him.'

Before Duffy could answer, Iron Eyes produced a match from one of his pockets and ignited it with a thumbnail. As he lit the cigar and drew in the smoke he stared at Jay.

'Sorry to disappoint you,' the bounty hunter said through a cloud of smoke. 'I'd delay digging a hole for me just yet. I don't die that easy.'

Brice Jay kept thinking about the handsome horse that he had assumed he would be able to claim for his own if its master were dead. He moved closer to Duffy as the soldier handed the opened whiskey bottle to Iron Eyes.

'What happened to this man?' he asked as he watched Iron Eyes drinking from the neck of the bottle.

'An arrow wound, Colonel,' the doctor replied. 'He was bleeding really bad. I reckon that's why he was unconscious when he rode into Fort Liberty.'

Brice Jay turned his head and looked long and hard at the bounty hunter. He could not understand how anyone who looked as savagely maimed as this creature did, could still actually be alive. He had seen many dead men during the numerous battles he had fought, but none of them looked as bad as this emaciated man. A cloud of smoke filled the air above Iron Eyes' head as his snake-like eyes darted between the three men who surrounded him.

The colonel glared at the wounded bounty hunter.

'What's your name?' Jay asked.

The bony hand pulled the bottle neck away from his lips and looked up at the colonel. He raised a torn eyebrow.

'My name is Iron Eyes,' he answered.

'Is that an Indian name?' Jay wondered.

Iron Eyes returned the cigar to his mouth and filled his lungs with its rancid smoke and shook his head. Most men who implied that he was any type of Indian usually lived to regret their question, but the bounty hunter knew that on those occasions he was in good enough shape to start a fight.

'It's just a name,' he said through a veil of smoke.

Trooper Casson looked up from the box of cigars when he heard the name and stepped closer to the prostrate figure on the table. He looked down at the bounty hunter and tilted his head before asking.

'Are you Iron Eyes the bounty hunter?' he asked. 'I've heard many tall tales about you.'

'Yep, I'm the bounty hunter,' Iron Eyes confirmed.

Brice Jay straightened up and looked at the trooper.

'Do you know this man, trooper?' he asked.

'No sir,' Casson said, but then added: 'But I've sure heard about him. Everybody's heard about this fella.

He's said to be the most dangerous critter that ever drew breath.'

Colonel Jay did not fully understand. He turned to the doctor and muttered.

'Have you ever heard of him, Duffy?'

The medical man continued his work, but nodded. 'Yep, I've heard about this critter over the years. I figured it was all hogwash, but if this fella reckons he's Iron Eyes, I sure ain't gonna argue with him.'

Brice Jay walked away from the three men and rested a hand on the door frame. His narrowed eyes studied the parade ground as he again thought about the horse which had carried the skeletal cargo into his fort. His only knowledge of the men who were called bounty hunters was that they hunted down outlaws and killed them for the reward money on their heads.

'Sit up,' Duffy told his patient. 'Now I have to clean and sew up the hole in your back.'

Jay looked back into the room. He watched as the horrifically scarred man with long lank hair managed to lever himself into a sitting position. A bead of sweat trailed down the colonel's face as he focused on the hideous sight. It was like observing a corpse rising from a grave in defiance of all that was holy. Even in his vivid imagination, Jay doubted that corpses could look that bad. Iron Eyes' face displayed every fight that he had endured over the years. The flesh clung to his skull as if it were a mask, and scars covered every visible inch of the face that stared hauntingly at the colonel.

A cold shiver traced down Jay's spine.

Iron Eyes showed no hint of pain as he continued to down the whiskey and fill his lungs with cigar smoke. As the doctor pulled the blood-stained trail-coat down to the bounty hunter's waist and methodically worked on his bony back, the colonel walked back to the table.

'Where did you get that horse?' he abruptly asked Iron Eyes.

The emaciated bounty hunter looked with unblinking eyes at the colonel as he savoured the flavour of the smoke as it crept back out of his mouth. He took another swig from the bottle and then exhaled at the floor.

'How come you're interested in my horse?' he whispered in a low, threatening tone. 'You ain't figuring on trying to steal that high-withered animal, are you? I'd kill anyone who tried to steal that horse.'

Brice Jay backed away from the threatening words. After composing himself he shrugged and then squared up to the bounty hunter.

'Have you a bill of sale for that stallion?' Jay snapped back at the bounty hunter.

Iron Eyes shook his head. His mane of long black hair sent droplets of sweat flying in all directions like a hound dog after it emerged from a waterhole.

'The varmint I got the horse from didn't give me a bill of sale, Colonel,' he hissed as he felt the needle being forced through his leathery skin.

'Why not?' Brice Jay pressed the bounty hunter.

'He was dead,' Iron Eyes snarled. 'I'd just killed the bastard. Does that satisfy you?'

61

Colonel Jay paced before the seated bounty hunter as both the trooper and the doctor looked on nervously. Then Jay stopped and pointed an accusing finger at Iron Eyes.

'Stealing horses is a hanging offence in this territory, Mr Iron Eyes.' He said. 'By your own admission, you obtained that palomino stallion by murdering its rightful owner.'

Iron Eyes lowered the bottle from his lips. Whiskey dribbled from the corners of his scarred mouth as he suddenly realized that he might be in trouble.

'What you getting at, old man?' he growled.

Jay looked across the room at the open-mouthed trooper. He gave a nod of his head and then moved to where he could see the Navy Colt gripped in the bounty hunter's claw-like grip.

'You are Iron Eyes the bounty hunter, correct?' Jay asked the monstrous man who watched him like a ravenous vulture.

'Sure I am,' Iron Eyes admitted. 'I already told you that.'

'You kill for a living?' Jay watched as the trooper quietly drew his pistol from his side holster and moved up behind the seated bounty hunter.

'That's what bounty hunters do,' Iron Eyes snarled as his finger curled around the trigger of the pistol at his side. 'I hunt down wanted critters that the law ain't got time to look for. I only kill men who are marked as wanted dead or alive.'

Jay nodded to Jody Casson.

The trooper moved to the side of the table where

Iron Eyes was sat as Duffy continued to sew the bounty hunter's skin together. Within seconds the young soldier raised his firearm and pressed it into the nape of Iron Eyes' neck.

'Don't you go moving a muscle, fella,' Casson warned.

A tortured smile graced the hideous face as he glared at Colonel Jay. As his prized Navy Colts were swiftly removed from him, Iron Eyes blew limp strands of hair off his face as he concentrated on the colonel.

'You really want my horse, don't you?' Iron Eyes rasped as the doctor concluded his work and moved away from his blood-stained patient.

Jay returned the smile and touched his temple.

'My compliments to you, Iron Eyes,' he said as the trooper moved away from the wounded bounty hunter. 'You catch on very quickly. What does a creature that looks like you want an obviously thoroughbred horse for? By your own admission, you killed its true owner. That fact alone could see you strung up by your scrawny neck.'

Iron Eyes removed the cigar from his mouth and tapped the ash at the floor. Whatever emotion was festering inside his mind could not have been better hidden. The lean bounty hunter remained apparently calm.

'You intend hanging me?' Iron Eyes asked through narrowed eyes as he watched the man before him like a mountain lion studying its prey.

Colonel Jay turned on his heels and paced slowly towards the door. As he reached it, he paused and looked back over his shoulder.

'Horse theft is a hanging offence,' Jay replied with a devious smirk on his face. 'The law is the law.'

Iron Eyes shook his head. He had encountered some of the most dangerous men ever to ride the vast ranges known as the Wild West, yet he had never met a man like Brice Jay before. He did not understand the veteran officer, but was determined to get the better of him, whatever it cost.

'You make it darn difficult to like you, old-timer,' he hissed through cigar smoke at the confident officer.

'I could hang you, but I've got a notion that you might be of use to me, Mr Iron Eyes,' Jay smiled. 'Unless you want to be hanged.'

Iron Eyes therefore guessed that the veteran cavalry officer had a plan for his future, but had no idea what it might be. He took another long swallow of the whiskey and allowed it to burn a trail down inside him.

'I've got no desire to be hanged again,' the gaunt bounty hunter drawled as whiskey dribbled from the corners of his mouth and dripped on to his lean chest.

Colonel Jay looked surprised.

'You've been hanged before?' he asked.

'Only the once,' Iron Eyes replied and raised his head to reveal the devilish mark around his neck. 'A lawman saved me before my neck snapped.'

The colonel cleared his throat.

'I've got a better use for you, Iron Eyes,' Jay sighed before adding, 'But if you decline my offer, I will have your stinking body hanging from a gallows by sundown tomorrow.'

Iron Eyes watched the officer leave the building and then took a long swallow from his whiskey bottle. As the fiery liquor burned its way down inside him, he brooded. He looked through cigar smoke at the trooper sat ten feet from him. The lamplight danced along the revolver in Casson's grip. The gun was aimed directly at him.

'Who is that fancy old-timer, soldier?' he asked.

'That's Colonel Brice Jay,' Casson answered. 'Why?'

The bony fingers put the cigar back between his razor sharp teeth and sucked in more smoke. As he slowly exhaled he looked at the trooper long and hard.

'I like to know the name of folks I intend killing,' Iron Eyes informed him. 'I'll teach that old-timer that it don't pay to ruffle my feathers.'

SEVEN

Like precious jewels set on a black velvet cloth, the stars twinkled as they had done for countless centuries in the vast, ever-moving night sky. Soon they would fade from the heavens as a new day announced itself and the blinding sun rose again over the desolate terrain.

An armed escort led three heavily chained soldiers into Jay's office, trailed by Sgt Leo Tolley. These were the deadliest enlisted men ever to face the colonel: he shifted papers off his ink blotter and listened to the rattling of their chains as they scraped on the polished wooden flooring. Brice Jay was all too aware that a new day was about to begin, but it would not break cover for at least another thirty minutes. By which time he would have completed his plan.

Colonel Jay glanced up from his desk and looked at the three prisoners, flanked by the two guards carrying rifles across their fronts. His eyes looked at Tolley and then back at the chained men, all of whom were awaiting the announcement of their death sentences.

'Are these the only prisoners who have been sentenced to death, sergeant?' he asked Tolley. 'I was hoping for a few more, but I imagine I should be grateful.'

'These are their names, sir,' Tolley placed a scrap of paper down before Jay and then stepped back as the colonel read the names of the prisoners. Jay looked up at the trio and sighed before returning his attention to the paper, which not only named them, but described the crimes they had been convicted for. Jay had never seen such a sickening array of charges before. All three were awaiting execution for various despicable crimes they had committed before Brice Jay had even arrived at Fort Liberty. The colonel inhaled sharply and stared at the men before him.

'It seems that my predecessor left me to deal with you boys,' he said tapping his fingers on the ink blotter. 'I imagine that you think my only choice regarding you three reprobates is deciding your ultimate fate. Should I have you hanged or perhaps placed before a firing squad?'

You could almost hear the nervous attempts at swallowing as Poke Spencer, Silas Kelly and Tom Peters stood before the veteran officer awaiting his decision. Brice Jay leaned back on his chair, then placed the fingers of his hands together and grinned at them. His watery eyes looked at the trio as his smile widened.

Poke Spencer was the oldest of the prisoners and had committed the more serious atrocities. His unshaven face screwed up as his fear turned to anger.

'Quit stalling and tell us how we're gonna die!' he

shouted at his superior as his shackles rattled. 'Are you gonna string us up or have us shot? Tell us!'

Kelly and Peters remained silent. They just stared at the floorboards and waited for Jay to announce how they were going to meet their Maker.

'Don't you go shouting at the colonel, Spencer,' Tolley growled at the prisoner with a shake of his clenched fist.

'Easy, sergeant!' Brice Jay chuckled and poured himself a large ration of brandy. As he sipped at the amber liquor he continued to watch the three very different prisoners. He placed the glass down and then stood and approached the men. The sound of his knee high boots echoed around the office. He moved close to the prisoners. There was no hint of fear in the commanding officer as he stopped before the snorting Spencer.

'What if I were to tell you that I have decided to offer you a chance of living rather than being executed?' Jay asked the men casually. Startled, Kelly looked up at the officer in stunned shock. Peters started to sob. Only Spencer seemed to be reluctant to believe Colonel Jay. As with all crooked men, he judged everyone to be as corrupt and evil as he was himself. He imagined that the seasoned officer was trying to trick them.

'What kinda trickery is this?' Spencer snarled. 'You're gonna kill us and you know it. We're doomed and there ain't no other way. Our court martials told us that. We're dead and you're as cruel as I am. Maybe even worse than me. I'd never have tormented anyone

I was intending to kill.'

Brice Jay stepped even closer to the angry Spencer.

'I'm offering you all a chance of living, Spencer,' he said in a cold and calculating tone. 'Take it or leave it. I have an offer which I hope you will consider.'

Spencer's expression changed. He suddenly understood that the colonel was serious. Deadly serious. The prisoner frowned.

'You mean it?' he gasped.

'Of course I mean it,' Jay nodded and stepped away from the men who were chained together like beasts of burden. He lifted his brandy glass to his lips and downed the entire contents of the satisfying liquor. 'I never josh about such important things like execution.'

Spencer fought against his restraints. 'I don't understand.'

'I'm going to send out a small troop of men to hunt for two missing females, Spencer,' Jay said as he placed the glass down on the blotter. 'I am looking for volunteers.'

The three shackled men looked at one another and then back at Jay as they absorbed the proposal. It was Spencer who was first to understand the gravity of the colonel's words.

'You're looking for men to enter them forested hills yonder and search for womenfolk?' he ranted fearfully. 'That's suicidal, Colonel.'

'Refusing is also suicidal, Spencer,' Jay noted wryly.

'Are them the gals that were taken by Red Feather?' Peters stammered nervously.

Jay nodded. 'I'm told by my spies that it was Red Feather who led his fellow warriors against the Smith family and absconded with the girls.'

Poke Spencer glanced at his fellow captives. 'I reckon that we've got a chance if we accept the colonel's offer, boys. It's gotta be better than getting hanged.'

'You're right. We've got nothing to lose.' Peters conceded. 'I just don't cotton to our chances against thousands of Injuns.'

Kelly looked at his fellow prisoners. 'We might survive and get back here with them females.'

Spencer glared angrily at Jay through his bushy eyebrows.

'It's loco but what choice have we got?' he hissed at the colonel. 'As long as you can guarantee that if we manage to bring them gals back here, we'll be free men.'

Jay nodded again.

'I take it that you accept my offer?' he enquired.

The prisoners all grunted in agreement.

Colonel Jay looked at the guards who flanked the three prisoners. 'Take these men to be cleaned up and given civilian clothes. Then make sure they get a solid meal in their guts. It might be a long time before they can get a square meal again.'

The guards saluted and led Spencer, Kelly and Peters out of the office as the first glimmers of daybreak spread across the parade ground.

The totally confused Sergeant Tolley moved to his commanding officer and whispered in his ear.

'If we arm them prisoners and let them leave the

fort they'll just scatter, Colonel,' the sergeant warned. 'We'll never see them again. How would you explain that to the authorities back east?'

Brice Jay opened the silver cigar case and removed a stout Havana from its interior. He clipped it and looked at Tolley, and shook his head in amused disagreement.

'Stop fretting, Leo,' he said. 'I doubt if any of them will live long enough to find their way back here. As far as I'm concerned they'll be as good as dead as soon as they ride out of Fort Liberty.'

Tolley shook his head. 'But they'll not head into Injun territory when you supply them with fresh horses and six-shooters. They'll turn and ride as fast and hard as they can to put as much distance between themselves and them Injuns, Colonel.'

Brice Jay shook his head and gave his underling a knowing smile. He then decided to confide in the fretting sergeant.

'They'll not be alone when they ride out from Fort Liberty, Leo,' he said. 'They'll have Iron Eyes leading them and he makes those three bastards look like angels.'

Tolley scratched his jaw. The name meant nothing to the loyal sergeant, who drew closer to the seasoned officer. He tilted his head and tried to comprehend what his superior was talking about.

'Who in tarnation is Iron Eyes?' he queried.

'You'll find out soon enough, Leo,' Jay replied as he scratched a match across the top of his desk and brought its flame to the tip of his cigar. As smoke filled his lungs the veteran cavalryman continued to smile before resting his hip on the edge of his desk. He then waved an open hand at the younger soldier. 'Go to the medical quarters and take Iron Eyes to the mess-room and make sure he fills his pitiful belly with a prime rib steak.'

'I still don't understand, Colonel.' Tolley admitted. 'Who exactly is this Iron Eyes critter?'

Brice Jay suddenly looked serious – deadly serious.

'He's a bounty hunter,' Jay informed. 'If I'm any judge of people I'd say that he's probably the most dangerous man I've ever encountered. Don't turn your back on him, and make sure that trooper Casson keeps his gun trained on him at all times. When he's fed and watered, bring him here to my office.'

'Is he going to lead the prisoners into Injun territory willingly, Sir?' Tolley wondered.

The smile returned to Jay's face.

'He doesn't even know that he's volunteered yet, Leo.' He laughed. 'But he has volunteered, and I think that if anyone can find and free those females, he can.'

'How can you be so certain?' the trooper had yet to meet the infamous bounty hunter and knew nothing about the calculated plotting behind the colonel's announcement.

The colonel stared through the cigar smoke as Tolley replaced his hat and straightened his tunic. He leaned forwards and winked at the trooper.

'How can I be so certain?' he repeated the innocent question as he tapped ash from his smouldering

Havana. 'Simple. It all hinges on a horse, Leo. A palomino stallion to be exact.'

Leo Tolley shook his head in befuddled confusion.

'A horse?' he repeated.

Jay stared through his cigar smoke.

'Exactly, Leo,' he said. 'A horse.'

EIGHT

The last drops of gravy were expertly mopped up by a chunk of bread, and then the gaunt bounty hunter rested his back against the spindles of his hardback chair and chewed. It was the first solid meal he had eaten in more than a month and it felt good. Yet even as he digested the food his mind was hatching a plan to get his precious Navy Colts back. Even half dead through lack of blood the notorious slayer of wanted outlaws was still far more dangerous that any of the enlisted troopers in the mess hall could ever imagine.

Iron Eyes had filled his deep pockets with long slender cigars before leaving the confines of the medical quarters, and as his eyes darted back and forth beneath his scarred eyelids he slowly plucked one of them from his pockets and pushed it between his teeth. He carefully observed the three men sharing the mess room with him. The cook had been woken up to prepare a meal for Iron Eyes, and was more asleep than awake. Trooper Casson was seated behind him, while Sergeant Tolley sat directly across

74

the table in front of him.

Even though Iron Eyes still looked more dead than actually alive, his strength was rapidly returning with every passing moment. Calmly he ignited a match with his thumbnail.

Across the table from Iron Eyes, Sergeant Tolley stared at the hideous sight of the man before him. Less than ten feet from them Casson still held his cocked revolver in his hands, trained on the bounty hunter's broad back.

Tolley could still not understand what was going on. The whole thing about this strange creature he had been told was called Iron Eyes seemed ludicrous to the soldier. Brice Jay had said that he was far more dangerous than the three prisoners he was about to lead into Indian territory, but Tolley found that difficult to accept. And if this skeletal bounty hunter was going to lead the small party of prisoners from Fort Liberty into the perilous forest, why was Colonel Jay so insistent that Casson kept his gun aimed on him? Iron Eyes didn't look threatening as he blew out the flickering flame of his match and casually tossed it over his shoulder.

Then suddenly Sergeant Tolley had the answer to the questions which tormented his tired mind. Without any warning the bounty hunter kicked the heavy table over, then as Tolley landed on his back with the weight of the table on top of him, he turned and jumped to his feet and in a mere heartbeat had leapt like a mountain lion at Casson and ripped the pistol from his hand. He smashed the back of his clenched fist across the trooper's jaw, sending him cart-wheeling, then emptied the army revolver and threw it at the feet of the dazed trooper. He then extracted his prized Navy Colts from the soldier's black belt and held them at hip level, one pointed at the soldier at his feet and the other aimed at the totally dazed Tolley.

Thus the notorious bounty hunter had just proved that the officer in command of Fort Liberty was totally correct in his comments regarding him. Even half dead, Iron Eyes was probably the most lethal man that any of them had ever encountered. He stood triumphantly above the pair of startled soldiers, and sucked in smoke as a cruel grin etched his brutalized face.

'Are you gonna kill us?' Tolley gulped fearfully.

'There ain't no profit in killing you,' Iron Eyes said through gritted teeth as he chewed on the cigar. 'I've wasted too much lead on them Injuns yonder.'

Tolley scrambled from under the hefty table and stared up at the formidable man standing with the Navy Colts in his bony grip. He had never been so afraid before.

'Then how come you got them six-shooters aimed at me and Casson?' Tolley heard himself ask.

Iron Eyes tossed his head back so that his long black hair rested on his coat collar. He then took a step towards the sergeant, who was struggling to his feet.

'Just my way of trying to stop you killing me,' he bluntly stated. 'Folks that look the way I do tend to draw bullets like flies to an outhouse.'

Tolley got to his feet and stared down the barrel of the six-shooter, which was aimed directly at him. He cleared his throat.

'Then why did you just do this?' he asked.

'That trooper had my Navy Colts,' Iron Eyes answered as he dropped one of the well-oiled weapons into one of his deep trail coat pockets. 'I don't cotton on to folks who get their hands on my weaponry.'

Leo Tolley brushed the sawdust off his uniform as the tall bounty hunter moved past him towards the door of the mess room. The soldier turned on his highly polished boots and watched as Iron Eyes paused by the closed door.

Both men stared at one another as Casson slowly clawed his way back to his feet and rested his spine against the wall.

'I'm waiting,' Iron Eyes growled at Tolley.

Tolley staggered toward the bounty hunter. 'What are you waiting for? You've got your guns back.'

Iron Eyes gave an amused grunt and lowered his six shooter so that it hung at his side. He shook his head.

'I ain't dumb enough to try and shoot my way out of this damn fort, trooper,' he growled. 'Besides, I'm running low on bullets.'

Tolley stopped in his tracks and glared up at the frighteningly tall bounty hunter.

'Then what do you want?' he asked wildly.

Iron Eyes reached down and grabbed the door knob and twisted it. A gust of warm morning air rushed through the gap and enveloped both men.

'I want you to take me to that old-timer,' the bounty hunter explained. 'The varmint that looks like he runs this fort.'

Leo Tolley rubbed the sweat off his brow as he stared at the figure who looked even more hideous in the rays of the morning sun. His voice stammered.

'You want to see Colonel Jay?' he asked.

Iron Eyes locked eyes with the frightened Tolley and shook his head slowly.

'Actually I wanna kill him, but I'll settle for seeing him to start with,' Iron Eyes whispered. 'Take me to his quarters right now.'

Tolley tried to swallow but there was no spittle.

NINE

The morning sun filled the vast parade ground and graced every structure within the boundary walls with its blinding light and increasing heat. Long shadows from the wooden walls of the fortress linked up with the equally elongated shadows of the numerous log structures contained within the safety of the fortress' boundaries. Sentries still walked along the high parapets with their rifles in readiness, even though none of the countless tribes' warriors had yet attacked the imposing fortress.

Though it was still early, Iron Eyes could feel the growing heat start to burn the exposed flesh of his face. He pulled up the ragged remains of his trail-coat collar as if trying to protect his already mutilated flesh.

'How you feeling, Iron Eyes?' Tolley asked the haunting figure, who walked a half-step behind him. It seemed impossible to the cavalry sergeant that anyone who had suffered the agony of being hit by an arrow only hours earlier could be capable of walking around as if nothing had happened. He looked back at the expressionless face that loomed ominously above him.

'I'm feeling OK, Shorty,' the bounty hunter whispered in a threatening hiss. 'Just keep walking. I wanna find that white-haired old-timer.'

'Why do you want to see the Colonel?' Tolley shrugged as they continued to reduce the distance between themselves and the officer's quarters.

Iron Eyes gave a grunt.

'That old critter is trying to steal my horse,' he snarled angrily as he pushed the soldier in the back. 'Nobody steals my horse. Not that big horse anyway. That high-withered critter has saved my life too many times for me to let anyone just take him from me.'

Tolley licked his dry lips. The sun was brutal as it beat down upon the two men. He looked back at Iron Eyes again, and wondered how the lean man had survived the numerous injuries that were evident across his emaciated body. With his torn shirt and ragged coat hanging like window drapes from his tortured frame, Iron Eyes was a walking dictionary of every battle he had fought. He wore the scars of each and every one of them.

'How long have you been hunting men for the price on their heads, Iron Eyes?' he asked carefully.

'Too long,' Iron Eyes quickly answered.

'By the looks of all them scars, you sure have earned your blood money,' Tolley nodded.

'I'm in better health than any of my enemies,' Iron Eyes retorted. 'They're all dead.'

The tall bounty hunter trailed Tolley towards the largest of the parade ground buildings; he hung on the shoulder of the sergeant ominously and easily matched the shorter man's pace.

'Do you always kill your enemies?' the sergeant enquired.

'Yep, I tend to kill them,' the gaunt figure replied. 'It don't pay to take prisoners in my line of work. That's why I need my horse. I ain't as fast as I used to be and that big stallion can outrun most things. Your colonel don't seem to understand how things work, out here in the wilderness.'

'You're right,' Tolley agreed. 'He ain't used to this kind of territory. Back east the Injuns have all but disappeared over the last twenty years. Colonel Jay has no idea that out here men have to live by a different code. Otherwise they end up as dead as your enemies.'

Iron Eyes abruptly stopped. A claw-like hand grabbed the soldier's shoulder and stopped Tolley in his tracks. He then turned the enlisted man around. Both men stared at one another for a few moments in the sun-baked parade ground.

'There ain't no Injuns back east?' Iron Eyes repeated Tolley's words. 'Where'd they go?'

Tolley shrugged. 'I don't know. Maybe they headed out here, or maybe they just got themselves killed.'

'Injuns don't like me,' Iron Eyes stated as he pushed Tolley back round, and both men resumed walking. 'Every damn Injun I've ever met has tried to kill me. It gets mighty tiresome.'

'Is that how you got yourself hit by an arrow?'

'Yep. They try to kill me and I have to kill them,' Iron Eyes sighed heavily. 'I hate killing Injuns. There ain't no profit in it. Bullets ain't cheap and I hate wasting them.'

With every step Tolley wondered if he was taking the infamous bounty hunter to kill the gallant officer he had faithfully served for years. Beads of sweat ran down from the soldier's hatband, but they had nothing to do with the rising heat.

Fear filled the soldier. Tolley had faced death many times during the war, but he had never before experienced anything quite like this.

As they neared the front of the officer's quarters the nervous sergeant abruptly stopped, turned, and looked up into the face of the living scarecrow. Tolley gritted his teeth before summoning every scrap of his courage.

'I don't understand what's going on between you and the colonel, Iron Eyes,' he said. 'But I can't take you in there and see you kill him.'

Iron Eyes tilted his head and stared down at the loyal trooper who was showing that he valued another's life more preciously than he did his own. His bony hand lowered his Navy Colt into his trail-coat pocket and he released his grip. The sound of the six-shooter rattling around with loose bullets filled the air.

'I'm not gonna kill your colonel,' he said. 'Not unless he tries to steal my horse.'

'Do you know why he wants your services, Iron

Eyes?' Tolley asked. 'He needs you. You're the only man who can do what needs to be done.'

The busted eyebrows rose up into the mane of unkempt hair as the words sank in. Iron Eyes placed a hand on the shoulder of the enlisted man.

'Sounds like that wily old colonel needs my help real bad,' he reasoned.

'He does.' Tolley confirmed. 'You're the only man in this territory who has a hope of succeeding.'

Iron Eyes had never been one to relish being smothered in flattery. Every sinew in his lean torso sensed that there was something he had not been told, and that angered the bounty hunter. His eyes burned into the shaking sergeant as he leaned over the smaller man.

'I'm the only man who can succeed at what?' he growled.

Tolley swallowed hard.

'There are two young females who need rescuing from them Injuns, Iron Eyes,' he blurted out. 'The Colonel figures that you being a skilled tracker, makes you perfect for the job.'

'What do them gals need rescuing from?' Iron Eyes asked as he bore down on the man in blue.

'Injuns,' Tolley croaked fearfully. 'A critter named Red Feather kidnapped two sisters and took them to his camp somewhere in the forest. Leastways, that's what we reckon.'

For a moment there was only silence in the vast fortress as the wounded bounty hunter thought about the words he had just heard. His face twitched as he pulled out a fresh cigar from one of his pockets and thoughtfully rammed it between his teeth. His bony fingers produced a match from another pocket and he ignited it with his thumbnail. As the flame flickered in the morning heat, his bullet-coloured eyes glanced down at the terrified trooper. Finally as he filled his lungs with the putrid smoke, he began to nod.

'Red Feather,' Iron Eyes said the name as though he were spitting out snake poison. 'I've tangled with him before. He's a real bad hombre and no mistake.'

'You've tangled with Red Feather?' Tolley gulped.

'Yep,' he confirmed. 'About four years back. I killed a half dozen of his braves before he high-tailed it. I thought he was gonna kill me, but I got lucky.'

'So you know where his camp is?' Tolley questioned.

Iron Eyes blew a long line of smoke at the ground and then nodded. His eyes narrowed as he stared ahead at the officer's quarters.

'Take me to your leader, Shorty,' he said. 'We've got business to talk over.

Both men entered the wooden structure.

TEN

The wall clock chimed to indicate that it was seven in the morning. Iron Eyes stared across the colonel's office from the comfort of a padded leather couch and yawned with boredom. To a man who had existed his entire life without ever seeing the point of clocks, the bounty hunter shook his head in total disgust. To Iron Eyes, it was either day or night. His narrowed eyes had watched the colonel for nearly a quarter of an hour since he had silently entered with Sergeant Tolley.

Brice Jay was busy signing papers at his desk and had yet to acknowledge the presence of the infamous bounty hunter, who glared at him like a ravenous wolf. This impressed Iron Eyes, for it showed the deadly hunter that the veteran commanding officer was totally unafraid of him.

After sucking the last remnants of smoke from his cigar, Iron Eyes dropped it on to the floorboards and crushed it under one of his mule-eared boots. The colonel intrigued the gaunt bounty hunter, for he had never encountered anyone quite like Jay before.

Colonel Jay was obviously still confident in his masculinity, even though he had lived long enough for his hair to turn snow white. That alone was a rarity in the wilds of the west. Yet unlike most men of his age, the decorated officer had retained his calm courage.

Iron Eyes admired the veteran man he had continued to stare at since his arrival in the officer's quarters. Most men half the colonel's age would have been intimidated but not Jay. Iron Eyes rubbed his dry mouth with the back of his hand and watched as Tolley tapped his knuckles on the office door and announced the arrival of another visitor.

Both Jay and the bounty hunter stared at the sergeant.

'Henry Smith is here, Colonel,' Tolley said.

Jay glanced up and nodded. The sergeant ushered the elderly Smith into the office and gestured to a hard chair opposite his own across the desk. Iron Eyes watched silently as the commanding officer rose from his seat and moved around the desk to be closer to the troubled father of the missing females.

'I'm sorry I turned up early, Colonel.' Smith sighed heavily. 'I just had to find out why you wanted to see me this morning after I've been trying to see you for weeks now.'

'Don't apologize, Smith.' Brice Jay said gruffly.

Smith looked up into the eyes of the man who was from the same generation as he was himself. The fingers of his hands interlocked before his trembling lips.

'I beg you not to keep me in suspense, Colonel,' he pleaded.

The tone in the man's shaking voice embarrassed the normally cool and collected officer. Jay inhaled deeply and then spoke calmly.

'I have decided to help you, Smith,' Jay announced as he rested his ancient bones on the edge of the desk and looked down at the equally aged man. 'I'm sorry for the long delay, but until this very moment I was unable to do so.'

Henry Smith looked up into the colonel's face with tears in his eyes as he rocked on the hardback chair. He could hardly contain himself. He was surprised by the short collection of words. Words he had been praying to hear for months since he had first arrived at Fort Liberty seeking help.

'You'll help me find my girls, Colonel?' he stammered.

Jay gave a firm nod of his head.

'Indeed,' he confirmed. 'I'm sorry for the delay, but now I can help you mount a search party to locate your beloved daughters.'

Smith leaned forward on his chair.

'What's happened to change things, Colonel?' he nervously asked. 'What's tipped the balance?'

Without uttering a word, Jay turned and then indicated with a hand in the direction of the resting Iron Eyes. Smith stood up and squinted at the seated bounty hunter before returning his attention to Jay.

'I don't understand,' he said truthfully.

'That, my friend, is the notorious gentleman

known as Iron Eyes,' Jay explained. 'He has agreed to lead a small party of men into the forest in search of your daughters.'

Smith scratched his whiskered face. The bounty hunter was not looking his best, with his long frame perched on the edge of the leather couch. There was no visible hint of the unique tracking skills which Iron Eyes possessed in abundance. The settler turned back to the colonel. Even though he was utterly grateful, Smith could not disguise his doubts.

'Him?' he mumbled. 'But he looks in a real bad way, Colonel.'

'Never judge a book by its cover, Smith,' Jay said. 'I can honestly tell you that Iron Eyes is the finest tracker ever to roam these barbaric lands.'

Smith glanced at the bounty hunter. 'If you say so.'

After listening to the unexpected praise, Iron Eyes quickly got to his feet and strode across the sunlit room towards the three men gathered by the desk. Tolley moved aside as the tall skeletal Iron Eyes closed in on the two elderly men. He paused by the desk and grinned at Smith.

'Believe the colonel, Smith,' Iron Eyes whispered. 'If I can't find them gals of yours, nobody can.'

The blunt words drew a smile from the settler.

'Thank you, son,' Smith managed to say. 'I'm sure you'll do your best, and for that, I'm eternally grateful.'

Iron Eyes nodded. His long black hair fell over his hideous features as he turned towards the colonel. Jay and Iron Eyes stared into one another's souls for a few moments.

'Me and the Colonel got us an agreement,' the bounty hunter said wryly. 'I help you, and he don't hang me.'

The expression on Henry Smith's face altered. His alarmed eyes flashed to Jay in search of an explanation.

'Iron Eyes is joking,' Brice Jay said. 'He has a very dry sense of humour.'

The bounty hunter raised a busted eyebrow. His bony hands picked up the brandy decanter and pulled out its glass stopper and sniffed its contents. The fumes of the expensive liquor filled his flared nostrils before he returned his attention back to the settler.

'Yeah, I'm just joking, friend,' he drawled.

Jay encouraged Smith to return to his seat, and then began to explain the situation. The seasoned officer knew that the elderly settler had to know every detail of the mission he had formulated.

'I'll explain my plan, Smith,' Jay started.

After a further twenty minutes the colonel had informed both Henry Smith and Iron Eyes of his detailed plan to send the small party of three prisoners and Iron Eyes into the forest to track down Loretta and Beth.

When the colonel had finished, Smith looked long and hard into Jay's military face. There was a determination in his face that only a fool would have disregarded.

'I'm going along with Iron Eyes and the three troopers, Colonel,' he stated firmly. 'I blame myself

89

for leaving my girls alone at my cabin. I should have taken them with me to get provisions, and that's been gnawing at my craw ever since. I can't expect folks like Iron Eyes here to risk their lives in Injun territory without taking the same risk myself.'

Brice Jay returned to his own chair.

'I'm not sure I can permit that, Smith. This is a very dangerous mission and if I can be blunt, you're not as young as we'd both like to be. I'm afraid that it might be too taxing for someone of your age.'

Henry Smith frowned.

Iron Eyes looked at Smith.

'You wanna risk your neck tagging along with me and the three varmints that the colonel has rustled up, Smith?' the bounty hunter asked before returning the stopper to the decanter.

Smith looked suddenly encouraged.

'I sure do, mister,' he said.

Iron Eyes turned his head and stared through the limp strands of black hair at the seated colonel.

'He's coming with me,' he said. 'He can watch my back should any of the three prisoners decide to add another notch to their gun grips.'

Reluctantly Brice Jay nodded in agreement. Before the colonel could say anything, Captain George Baker entered the outer office and marched towards the wide open door to the colonel's inner sanctum.

All three men looked at Baker.

'I've just heard about the rescue mission you're planning on sending out into the heart of Indian country, Colonel,' Baker said as he removed his hat and held it over his belt buckle. 'I'd like to volunteer to go along.'

Jay nodded. 'OK, Captain. You can go along with Iron Eyes and the rest of the boys.'

Iron Eyes placed a fresh cigar between his lips and looked at the seated colonel as he scratched a match along the top of the desk. He cupped its flame and puffed thoughtfully.

'So that makes six of us heading out into that forest yonder, Colonel,' he said through a cloud of smoke. He dropped the spent match into the ashtray beside Jay and looked down at his blood-stained clothes. 'I need a new shirt and a new trail coat. I want four bottles of whiskey in my saddle-bags and two boxes of ammunition for my Navy Colts. That's what it'll cost for me to head back into them trees.'

Jay smiled and nodded.

'Agreed,' he said. 'I'll have six fresh horses tied up outside here just before sundown. You will leave Fort Liberty under the cover of darkness. I suggest you all take advantage of the hours of daylight and get some sleep. I doubt that any of you will have time to sleep once you enter that forest.'

Iron Eyes looked at the veteran colonel.

'I got me a feeling that my high-withered palomino ain't gonna be one of them nags, Colonel,' he said.

'I shall return your horse to you when you return from your mission, Iron Eyes,' Brice Jay said before leaning back on his chair. 'It will be well looked after in your absence.'

With the slender cigar gripped firmly between his

razor sharp teeth, Iron Eyes moved to the window and stared out into the blinding sunlight. He exhaled a line of grey smoke and glanced over his wide, bony shoulder at the seated Jay.

'I want a red shirt, Colonel,' he hissed. 'Red don't show the bloodstains as quickly as most other colours. I got me a feeling in my guts that we'll all be spilling plenty of blood before this is over.'

The four men behind the bounty hunter said nothing. They knew that the haunting figure was right. His chilling words would remain with them for as long as they drew breath.

ELEVEN

Two heavily armed sentries remained outside the military jailhouse as the three prisoners in their new civilian trail gear pondered their fate. The trio of reluctant volunteers sat inside the small, sweltering cell and watched the bright stream of sunshine carve its way from the barred window across its stinking confines. They were well used to the unholy heat, but it wasn't that which made them sweat like pigs.

It was the thought that soon they would be forced to leave the relative safety of Fort Liberty and head straight into the surrounding forest. A forest which they knew harboured an untold number of hostiles. Colonel Jay had offered them this chance of evading the executioner's wrath, but it was a slender hope.

Each of the murderous trio had been awaiting execution for what seemed an eternity, yet now a hangman's knot or a firing squad seemed preferable to facing the Indians, who had grown in number during the previous few months. The Indians were on the warpath, and would show no mercy to anyone who entered the forest, and the prisoners were well aware of that simple fact. Yet neither Spencer, Kelly nor Peters wanted to remain in the fortress and await certain death. Their minds raced as fear grew in their bellies and mocked their helplessness.

They had said very little since being brought back to the confines of the cell from the mess hall. Their bellies were full with what each of them suspected might be their final meal – but they no longer wore the shackles that they had trailed around since being sentenced to death.

Spencer had been brooding over their plight since the guards had escorted them back to the jail-house. His devilish mind had been considering every option that might present itself to them when they left the fort. Unlike his cohorts, Spencer was a cruel killer, yet he had a keen imagination. He alone would take advantage of the slightest of chances to escape, if it presented itself. He kept telling himself that at least the Indian-infested terrain offered them a glimmer of hope. To remain in Fort Liberty was certain death.

As the most senior of the prisoners desperately tried to plot a way of surviving the mission Colonel Jay had thought up, his fellow prisoners were becoming more and more terrified. Confidence was draining rapidly from both Kelly and Peters faster than the sweat that had already drenched their trail gear. The younger prisoners moved their crude stools closer to Spencer and stared pathetically at him, like sinners awaiting deliverance.

'Don't crowd me, boys,' Spencer growled at them. 'I'll figure out a plan before we leave this damn fort.'

'I got me a gnawing in my craw that one way or another, we'll be buzzard meat as soon as we enter them trees,' Kelly said, shaking his head as Peters rose to his feet and walked to the stout wooden door. The youngest of the three men pressed his ear to the door frame and listened. He could hear the guards talking in the corridor outside the small jail cell.

Both Spencer and Kelly stared at Peters. They could not understand what had drawn his attention as they, too, rose to their full height and moved towards the attentive prisoner. Spencer was about to speak when Peters raised a hand to silence any questions. Then after a few moments the sweat-soaked young prisoner moved away from the door and stood in the bright rays of the sun.

'Them guards sure talk loud,' Peters said as he rubbed his unshaven jaw.

Poke Spencer and Silas Kelly moved to the shoulders of their comrade.

'What did them bastards say, Tom?' Spencer snorted.

'They was talking about some critter named Iron Eyes,' Peters replied. 'It seems that he's gonna lead us into them trees, boys.'

'He must be plumb loco,' Spencer spat.

'Iron Eyes?' Kelly looked bewildered. 'I've never heard of him.'

'I have,' Spencer grunted.

'Who is he?' Kelly probed.

95

Spencer grabbed the shoulder of the youngest condemned man and pulled him closer. He snarled into
Peters' ear.

'What did them guards say about Iron Eyes, Tom?'
he pressed.

Peters bit his lower lip. 'They reckoned that the
colonel threatened Iron Eyes with hanging if he
didn't lead a search party into them Injun lands. That
varmint is being blackmailed to search for them Smith
gals, just like us.'

'Who in tarnation is Iron Eyes?' Kelly shrugged as
his eyes darted between both his fellow prisoners.
'Sounds like an Injun to me.'

'He ain't no Injun,' Spencer asserted as his
clenched fist smacked into the palm of his hand. Kelly
and Peters looked at the muscular Spencer. It seemed
that he alone knew exactly who the mysterious Iron
Eyes was.

'Iron Eyes is a bounty hunter, Silas,' Spencer spat.
'They say that once he's on your tail, you're a dead
man. He's the meanest varmint ever to roam this or
any other territory.'

'What did them guards say this Iron Eyes did to be
threatened with hanging, Tom?' Kelly wondered as he
stared at Peters. 'If he's so damn tough I'd have
figured that he'd just laugh off any threats the
Colonel might throw at him.'

Peters chuckled to himself. 'It seems that the
bounty hunter has got himself a real fine horse and
the Colonel wants it for his own. That's what them
guards said anyway. It seems that Iron Eyes ain't got a

bill of sale for the nag.'

Spencer grinned.

'Blackmail,' he laughed. 'It seems that the colonel ain't no better than us. He wants Iron Eyes' horse and unless that bounty hunter knuckles under, he'll get hanged.'

'Just like us,' Kelly sighed.

The smile evaporated from Spencer's face. He paced around the confines of the jailhouse cell thoughtfully. He had heard the tales of the notorious bounty hunter and wondered if any of them could actually be true.

'Why would someone as ornery as Iron Eyes be bullied by the Colonel, Poke?' Peters asked the older prisoner.

'You forget that Colonel Jay has hundreds of men to do his fighting for him,' Spencer sighed. 'Even Iron Eyes ain't dumb enough to tackle them kinda odds.'

'But he's dumb enough to lead a few men into them trees yonder,' Kelly rested his knuckles on his belt. 'Them trees is crawling with Injuns. Who knows how many Injuns. I've heard talk that the Navaho and the Cheyenne and a whole bunch of other tribes have joined forces, Poke. Iron Eyes is willing to lead us against them?'

'He ain't willing,' Spencer argued. 'He's been threatened with execution if he don't do what that crusty old fossil tells him. He's in the same cooking pot as us.'

The faces of the two younger prisoners suddenly went ashen as the gravity of their upcoming plight dawned on them.

'We're as good as dead, Poke,' Kelly spat at the floor.

'The more I think about it,' Peters shrugged, 'the more I reckon we ain't got a hope in hell.'

Poke Spencer grunted with amusement, and nodded. 'We'll get away, boys. Mark my words, as soon as that Iron Eyes turns his back on us, I'll fill it with lead. We'll be two states away from here before Colonel Jay realizes we're gone.'

'You reckon Iron Eyes can be killed that easy?' Kelly asked the older of the trio.

Spencer raised an eyebrow.

'Iron Eyes?' he repeated the name. 'He's just a man like every other man I've tangled with. They all die. He ain't no different to any of them.'

Peters moved closer to Spencer.

'Them guards were saying that he ain't like other men, Poke,' he stammered. 'They was saying that Iron Eyes ain't even alive like you and me. They said that he's some kinda monster that the Devil cooked up to torment regular folks.'

Spencer grunted with laughter.

'There ain't no such thing as monsters, boy,' he insisted.

'Them guards sounded plumb scared,' the wide-eyed Peters said. 'They'd seen him close up, and he's like a corpse covered in scraps of skin. They said he was drenched in his own blood, but it didn't seem to make no difference to him. They give him a cigar and a bottle of whiskey and he refused to die like regular folks. No normal critter looks or acts like that, Poke.'

Thoughtfully, Spencer moved back to the small window. His hands gripped the iron bars as he squinted out into the parade ground.

'He's a bounty hunter. Some say he's the most dangerous bastard ever to ride in these parts,' he grunted in a tone designed to settle his cohorts' nerves. 'Most of that blood them guards were talking about was probably spilled by the outlaws he's gunned down.'

Kelly and Peters looked at each other. Spencer might have been right about the blood, they both thought.

'Yeah, that sounds right,' Kelly shrugged.

'Sure it is, Silas.' Spencer sighed. Then he caught a fleeting glimpse of a strange man striding across the vast area of sand. He released his grip on the bars and then cupped his hands around his eyes in a vain attempt to focus on the unholy sight. His mouth fell open as Iron Eyes walked from view into the large livery stables.

Peters was first to notice the startled expression carved into Spencer's face as he turned away from the window and sat down on his small three-legged stool.

'What's wrong, Poke?' he asked. 'You look like you just seen a ghost.'

There was no answer.

Both Kelly and Peters edged closer to the seated Spencer, yet the older man seemed oblivious to them as he looked blankly through the shaft of sunlight into the gloom of the cell.

'You OK, Poke?' Peters asked the dumbstruck

figure, who just sat staring across the wooden jail-house. He shook Spencer's shoulder. 'Poke?'

'Are you OK?' Kelly asked the normally cold, calcu-lating Spencer. Neither of the younger prisoners had ever seen him look so stunned before. It troubled them.

Finally, Spencer drew in breath and shivered as he became aware of the two concerned prisoners stand-ing above him. He blinked hard and looked at them.

'What? Are you two numbskulls talking to me?' he asked, glancing at them both in turn. Tom Peters nodded, and leaned closer to the ashen-faced Spencer.

'I said you look like you just seen a ghost, Poke,' he repeated.

Spencer stroked his unshaven jaw thoughtfully. He had seen many things in his murderous past, but nothing like the sight of the dishevelled bounty hunter. Every tall story he had heard about the infa-mous Iron Eyes now seemed understated.

'Maybe I just did,' he said.

'Did what?' Peters questioned.

'Maybe I did just see a ghost,' Spencer grunted.

Fear now flowed freely like sweat from all three men as they sat in the stinking jail cell awaiting their fate. The sight of Iron Eyes was branded into the mind of Poke Spencer, and it would remain there for as long as the brutal killer sucked in air. But the horrific sight was not so easily forgotten, ever.

TWELVE

The heart of Fort Liberty was like a cauldron during the hours of daylight. The heat could rise to unimaginable temperatures during the summer months, and to sleep was an impossible command for the men who awaited sundown. Colonel Jay might have been able to catch a few hours of rest himself, but none of the men who were about to undertake the perilous mission to rescue the Smith sisters could do anything apart from fretting.

Only the dishevelled bounty hunter managed to ignore the overwhelming heat and sleep throughout the afternoon. He had given the army blacksmith a silver dollar and headed up into the stable loft moments after being observed by Poke Spencer from the jailhouse window. For eight long hours the gaunt Iron Eyes slept amid piles of hay with his fingers curled around the triggers of his precious Navy Colts.

Iron Eyes had been oblivious to the busy stables activities and every other noise which drifted through the sweltering loft as his emaciated body rested in readiness for the coming trek he and the others were about to undertake.

As the sun finally set beyond the trees and shadows

suddenly filled the fortress, the deadly Iron Eyes awoke from his long sleep and glanced around the high loft. When he recalled where he was, his legendary honed senses relaxed. The lean man rose to his full height and slid his guns back into his cigar- and bullet-filled pockets.

From his high vantage point, Iron Eyes stared out into the centre of the parade ground as its lanterns were slowly lit around the shadowy area. He rested a bony hand on the frame of the stable window and spat. Before the spittle hit the sand far below he had pulled out a long cigar and placed it between his razor-sharp teeth.

Darkness crept stealthily across the large fortress as the narrowed eyes of the bounty hunter watched unseen. He watched the sentries pacing around the high parapet with their rifles in readiness for a potential attack. He grunted to himself and turned away. The belly of the large livery stable glowed in amber light as its lanterns were lit. His large blood-stained spurs rattled as his thin legs took him to the ladder, and he quickly climbed back down into the heart of the main part of the stable. His eyes tightened as he looked around the vast interior of the livery stable, and he stopped when he saw his prized palomino stallion in a stall nearby.

Iron Eyes strode to the stalled animal and looked the sturdy creature up and down. A dozen or more cuts and grazes still covered the horse's legs and bore proof of the fearless stallion's courage. The high-withered animal moved closer to its master as Iron Eyes silently nodded at the creature.

For countless years the bounty hunter had ridden mainly Indian ponies which he had not treated kindly. He had never cared for horses until he obtained the palomino, but the magnificent stallion had been totally different to the dozens that had preceded it. The animal had more speed than any other horse he had ever encountered, and had saved its master several times since he had first acquired it.

Iron Eyes ran a bony hand along the neck of the alert stallion as one of the liverymen moved towards him. The haunting bounty hunter turned his head swiftly and stared through the limp strands of hair at the approaching man.

The blacksmith was carrying a small bundle in his hands.

'What you got there?' Iron Eyes rasped as he chewed on the end of the cigar.

'These are some fresh clothes,' the blacksmith said, holding out the parcel to the brutalized bounty hunter. 'The Colonel had them sent over here for you.'

The expression on the face of Iron Eyes remained exactly the same as he accepted the bundle. He quickly ripped open the brown paper and string and stared at the new trail gear. A red shirt and a brand new trail coat greeted his eyes. He looked down at his own blood-stained cloths.

Iron Eyes gave a nod of his head but remained silent as he removed his bloody coat and tattered shirt. He then donned their replacements in quick time. His long bony fingers transferred everything from his deep coat pockets including his lethal pair of six-shooters and the loose bullets. When the last of his cigars were placed in his pockets he looked up at the burly liveryman who had remained close to the pitifully lean man during the exercise.

'You sure are carrying a lot of scars, Mister,' the big man said rubbing the sweat from his face. 'I ain't never seen so many scars before.'

'Folks tend to shoot at me,' the bounty hunter said.

'It looks like most of them found their target,' the liveryman grunted. 'You sure should learn how to duck.'

As Iron Eyes scratched a match with his thumbnail and raised it to the twisted cigar in his mouth the muscular man dutifully picked up the discarded clothes.

'Who in tarnation are you, Mister?' the nervous man asked.

'I'm Iron Eyes,' he said through a line of smoke.

The trooper had heard the name from the numerous other cavalrymen who milled in and around the livery stables. He gritted his teeth and stared straight at the haunting figure before him.

'Are you the critter that palomino carried in here last night?' the trooper asked as he carried the clothing toward the forge and tossed them on the red hot coals. 'I heard that you was more dead than alive.'

'A bottle of whiskey cured me,' Iron Eyes said drily.

The large man watched the rags burning and then turned his attention back to the tall bounty hunter. He bit his lip and then ventured.

'Are you seriously going to try and track down them Smith gals?' he enquired anxiously. 'They reckon that Red Feather took them Smith gals as trophies, Iron

Eyes. He ain't gonna give them back without a fight. Nobody knows how many Injuns are roaming around them forests. It's certain death riding in there.'

Iron Eyes gave a nod of his head. His long mane of hair floated in the lantern light as he inhaled more cigar smoke and moved away from the palomino.

'I figured that out on my lonesome,' he said as he stared out of the large barn doors into the starlight. 'Red Feather is the son of Fire Mountain. He's bad medicine.'

'You know about them Sioux warriors?' the muscular stableman asked. 'And you're still figuring on trying to rescue them gals?'

'I'm gonna try to bring them gals back,' Iron Eyes shrugged and walked out of the large stable building with the cigar gripped between his teeth. A line of smoke trailed the bounty hunter. 'If it comes down to a fight, they'll soon learn that I'm as bad they are. Maybe even worse.'

The liveryman shook his head as Iron Eyes walked away from the livery stable. The eerie light of the stars high above the fort gave the infamous bounty hunter an even more horrific appearance – painfully lean, Iron Eyes looked more like a ghost than usual as his mane of black hair clung to the pale flesh of his face.

Iron Eyes glanced upwards through the cigar smoke that filtered through his gritted teeth. The sky was angry. Black storm clouds raced across the heavens, blotting out all but the most determined of stars. He felt a few spots of rain touch his lank hair, and grunted angrily as he turned the corner and headed towards the main building.

'At least the weather's on my side,' he rasped as he began to concentrate on the gruelling mission he was about to embark upon. 'What I need right now is a good old-fashioned thunderstorm.'

His scarred eyes looked up through the fine rain and tightened in his skull. As the gaunt bounty hunter got close to the officers' quarters, he noticed that there were seven well-rested saddle horses tethered outside the wooden structure. The number of mounts did not tally with the number of riders he had been told were going to embark on the deadly quest. Iron Eyes pulled the cigar from his mouth as he curiously pondered on why there was an extra mount secured to the hitching rail outside the impressive structure.

Bathed in the glowing lantern light which cascaded from the building's large windows and spread across the horses, the bounty hunter moved between the tethered cavalry mounts and checked each of their saddle-bags in turn. He continued inspecting the leather satchels until he found the one he was seeking. The one with a box of ammunition for his Navy Colts and four bottles of whiskey nestling in the bags.

A satisfied smirk spread over his mutilated features as he secured the bags' buckles. He tugged at the restraining long leathers and led the horse away from the others and checked it carefully. It was bigger than the Indian ponies he had once ridden, but nowhere near as powerful as his golden palomino. Only the thought of how dangerous it was in the depths of the forested hills made the notorious bounty hunter happy that he was not taking his own prized stallion back into the land he knew was infested with untold numbers of Indians.

His bony hand tossed the cigar at the wet sand. He was still checking the cavalry horse when he heard a sound coming from within the large wooden building behind his wide shoulders. Iron Eyes slowly turned and stared through the falling rain at the sturdy door.

The door flew open. Lamplight spread out from the main building and illuminated the tall bounty hunter in its amber glow. His unblinking eyes appeared to glow like red-hot coals as they observed the strange assortment of men coming out.

The statue-like Iron Eyes stood holding the horse's reins as Colonel Brice Jay escorted the men who were going to accompany the bounty hunter out into the parade ground. None of the prisoners looked as if they could be trusted, and the renowned hunter of men knew that he would have to be mighty careful if he wanted to survive this already suicidal mission.

'I see that you are ready to start your valiant quest, Iron Eyes,' Jay said as Spencer, Kelly and Peters walked to their allotted mounts. Iron Eyes gave a nod of his head as his eyes burned through the falling rain and watched the murderous trio.

'This bunch of vermin don't look the kind of critters you want to turn your back on, Colonel,' Iron Eyes hissed like a coiled rattler as he studied Spencer and his cohorts. 'I sure hope they remember that I'm on their side.'

'We know whose side we're on, Iron Eyes,' Poke Spencer grunted to the lean bounty hunter.

Iron Eyes forced a smile at the trio of hardened killers.

'Just remember that I'm your ticket out of that forest, gents,' he growled. 'Without me you'll all get your scalps lifted. We need every man possible to fight off them Injuns, so try not to shoot in my direction.'

Kelly, Spencer and Peters said nothing as they stared angrily at the hideous man before them and considered his stark warning.

Colonel Jay ushered the three other men towards the tethered horses, and then concentrated his attention on Iron Eyes. The veteran soldier could not understand the sullen creature who stood before him. Jay thought that he had encountered every known variety of man during his military service, but nothing had prepared him for anyone like Iron Eyes.

By all accounts the bounty hunter should be dead or at least flat on his back recovering from his severe injuries. It seemed impossible that anyone who had been so close to death less than twenty-four hours earlier could be actually standing defiantly before him – but that was exactly what the bounty hunter was doing.

Iron Eyes raised his hand and then pointed at the colonel.

'When I get back I'm taking my palomino and riding out of here, Colonel,' he hissed at the commanding officer. 'Like I told you, if you try to trick me I'll surely kill you.'

Jay cleared his throat. 'No tricks. I swear to you.'

Iron Eyes then glanced curiously at the three other

men who had followed the prisoners out into the drizzle and begun to untie their mounts. With his reins gripped in his claw-like hand he looked back at Jay in search of answers.

'Who are these varmints again?' he asked with a gesture of his free hand as one by one they mounted.

Brice Jay pointed a hand at Smith and then the cavalrymen.

'This is Henry Smith. It is his daughters that were taken by the Indians,' he explained. 'Captain Brown has volunteered to undertake this journey with you.'

Iron Eyes looked at Sergeant Tolley.

'I'm kinda surprised that you're tagging along with us,' he said bluntly to the trooper. 'I'd have figured that you got yourself a real soft deal going by being the colonel's right-hand man.'

'I volunteered for this mission just like Captain Brown,' Tolley said.

'Are you sure you wanna tag along?' Iron Eyes asked. 'This is going to be mighty dangerous.'

'Leo fought beside me in many campaigns, Iron Eyes,' Colonel Jay said proudly. 'There is no braver man in the cavalry. You'll find that he is the equal of anyone in this fortress, and probably superior when it comes to courage.'

Iron Eyes nodded at Tolley. 'Guard my back, Leo. I'm a tad nervous of having them convicted murderers in our happy little group.'

Tolley looked to Spencer and his fellow convicts and then returned his attention to the bounty hunter.

'Don't you go fretting, Iron Eyes,' he said. 'They'll

not turn their guns on you with me behind them. I've killed bigger and better varmints than them.'

Poke Spencer stared at the sergeant.

'We'll not turn on any of you boys,' he grunted.

'There'll be more than enough folks to aim your guns at when we enter them trees without killing one another,' Iron Eyes said before adding. 'Those Injuns don't take prisoners unless they're womenfolk. They tend to kill us men just for the sheer pleasure of it. We need every one of us to have a hope of surviving this.'

The colonel cleared his throat and then watched as the six men stepped into their stirrups and mounted their horses. Only Iron Eyes remained at the head of his allocated horse. He moved closer to Smith and looked up at the veteran.

'We'll find them girls of yours, Smith,' he told the settler in a low whisper, 'but I'll need your help tracking them down.'

'I'll help you as best I can, Iron Eyes,' Smith said with a slow nod of his head. 'I'm old, but if it's the last thing I do, I want to rescue my daughters.'

The bounty hunter nodded and then grabbed the saddle horn and hauled himself up on to the cavalry mount. He gathered up his reins, and then stared at the six mounted men beside him. It was the first time he had ever led so many people into hostile territory, but he gave no hint of his own trepidations.

Iron Eyes noted that each of the men was clad in fresh trail gear just like himself. His bony hands swung the horse around so that it faced the stout fortress gates.

'Give them convicts their guns,' he told Baker. 'They'll surely need them when we reach the trees.'

Captain Baker looked down at the Colonel.

'Do as Iron Eyes instructed you, Captain,' Brice Jay instructed the junior officer.

Baker nodded and did as the bounty hunter ordered, cautiously handing over the three .45s to the trio of convicts who holstered them as they turned their mounts.

Iron Eyes looked over his wide shoulder at the six faces and then gave a firm nod of his head.

'Let's ride, boys,' he said tapping his spurs into the flanks of the horse beneath him. The seven horses started towards the gates. Colonel Brice Jay raised his right arm and signalled to the sentries on the gates. The two men slowly opened the twin gates as the horsemen neared them.

The riders rode out of Fort Liberty at a slow, steady pace and headed towards the distant trees. The rain continued to fall as Iron Eyes led the six horsemen across the cleared ground towards the forest. Henry Smith rode a few paces behind the bounty hunter with the three convicted men a yard or so behind him. Baker and Tolley brought up the rear of the small troop and watched the prisoners carefully.

The captain and the sergeant knew that Spencer, Kelly and Peters were not to be trusted. They held their six-shooters in their hands in readiness. If any of the trio were to unexpectedly draw their newly acquired weaponry from their holsters, Baker and Tolley would shoot them.

111

As the horsemen rode through the driving rainfall Colonel Jay watched from the parapet as the gates were secured below his lofty perch. The seasoned commanding officer was in two minds as to the mission. Half of him wanted them to succeed and bring the Smith sisters back to the safety of Fort Liberty, while his other half still desired the magnificent palomino stallion he knew he could only obtain if Iron Eyes were killed. Jay continued to watch the group of riders as they left the relative safety of Fort Liberty and travelled on towards the perilous forest.

The rain grew harder as black clouds blotted out the stars above their heads. He sighed and wondered if he would ever see any of the horsemen again.

Two of the sentries moved along the wooden parapet and stood on either side of the expressionless Jay. Both stared out through the falling rain as the horsemen slowly began to disappear from view.

'They're either the dumbest critters at Fort Liberty or the bravest,' one of the guards commented.

Brice Jay said nothing.

The other rifle-clutching guard rested the barrel of his weapon on the pointed top of the wall and shook his head in a mixture of admiration and pity.

'Do you reckon they'll save them gals and get back here, Colonel?' he asked his commanding officer. 'Some say there's more Injuns in that forest than fleas on a hound's back. I'd sure not gamble on any of them surviving.'

Every fibre of Brice Jay's body shivered as the rain started to find its way into his uniform collar. He adjusted his hat, and without answering, turned away from the troopers. He carefully made his way back down to the parade ground when the trooper repeated his question.

'Do you, Colonel?' the cavalryman called out from high above Jay. 'Do you reckon they'll save them gals and get back here?'

Jay glanced through the rain at the enlisted man.

'To be frank, I'm not sure,' he replied.

The parapet sentries watched as the colonel carefully made his way back across the parade ground towards the lantern-lit building.

Both troopers looked back over the fortress wall into the darkness to where they had last seen the seven riders. The driving rain and cloud-covered sky cast a blanket of darkness over the cleared ground between Fort Liberty and the forest, making it impossible for either of the men to see the horsemen any longer.

'None of them will come back, Jeb,' the first sentry said as he pulled up the collar of his tunic against the rain.

'You could be right, Dan,' his equally soaked companion agreed thoughtfully. 'A month back, the last patrol barely escaped them trees with their hair, if you recall.'

'Yeah, and there was more than twenty of them,' Trooper Dan reminded his companion.

'There weren't twenty of them when that patrol returned from them trees yonder, Dan,' the trooper remembered the state of the cavalrymen when they managed to escape the Indians' wrath. 'I think there

113

was less than ten troopers left, and half of them were wounded.'

Both soldiers straightened up and faced in opposite directions in readiness to march along the high walkway. With rain battering their faces they began their well practised march along the parapet.

The sound of the growing storm began to howl like a pack of timber wolves across the fortress. None of the many souls within its confines gave a second thought to the seven riders as they steered their horses into the forest.

Only the two drenched guards who had witnessed the departure of Iron Eyes and his motley crew gave the seven horsemen a fleeting thought as they slowly moved along the walkway.

Colonel Brice Jay returned to his private quarters and unbuttoned his tunic before removing it and sitting on the edge of his cot. He eased off his black boots, and then poured himself a glass full of fragrant brandy. As the fumes filled the room he lay back against his pillows and looked up at the ceiling.

A cruel smile lit up his face in the candlelight.

Jay was not the first commanding officer to send men into the jaws of almost certain death, and he knew that he would not be the last. He lifted the glass, tasted the liquor and then swallowed its contents in one swift action.

He closed his eyes and was asleep before the warm brandy had even made its way down inside him.

THIRTEEN

White flashes erupted in the black clouds above the seven horsemen as they rode through the driving rain towards the wall of black trees. As splinters of rod lightning crackled through the growing mayhem, the bedraggled bounty hunter glanced back at the men who were steering their mounts in his wake.

Iron Eyes led his six followers into the forest and then pulled his reins up to his chest. He turned in his saddle and watched as the riders trailed him into the edge of the forest and stopped around his bedraggled mount. The open ground between the fort and the trees was dark as the clouds rumbled angrily above the cleared ground – but it was nowhere as dark as it was inside the daunting woodland.

As lightning forked across the sky and momentarily lit up the ghostly trees that encircled them, Iron Eyes studied their expressions. The three condemned men sat silently watching the horrific bounty hunter with a shared evil expression on their wet faces. Most men might have been troubled by the fact that he sensed that they were planning to kill him and escape, but not Iron Eyes.

Iron Eyes had faced too many men cut from the same cloth as these three, and had grown used to it over the years. Fear was something he had outgrown a long time ago. Death was a constant companion to the savagely mutilated bounty hunter, and he knew that it rode on his shoulder. There is nothing a man can do to prevent the Grim Reaper choosing to take you when it is your time to die.

Those who fear the coming of death die a thousand times.

The expression on the faces of the two troopers was different to that of the convicts. They just watched the three convicted killers, knowing that if they did attack their companions in a bid to flee, they would have to turn their guns on them as quickly as possible.

Only the face of the aged Henry Smith bore any resemblance to that of someone who had nothing on his mind apart from trying to find and free his precious daughters. Iron Eyes knew that Smith was sincere and desired only to locate his daughters and lead them to a place of safety.

The rain continued to lash the sodden ground behind them with a ferocity which the bounty hunter knew would get worse before it got better. Momentarily the entire forest lit up as a thunderclap exploded directly above them. Their mounts shied but were kept in check as the smell of sulphur filled the ground which surrounded them.

Iron Eyes ran his bony fingers through his wet hair

and pushed it off his haggard features as he studied the men behind his wide back again. It was as though he were daring the trio of deadly men to attempt to kill him. He knew that none of the murderous three horsemen would meet his silent challenge, for like all killers they preferred their victims to be weak or help-less.

Iron Eyes said nothing as he turned back and stared across the head of the horse beneath him into the forest. The open ground was dark, but nothing like the depths of the forested hills before him. He gritted his teeth as his left hand searched for a cigar which was not as wet as the rest of his emaciated body.

Henry Smith moved his mount closer to the bounty hunter and drew rein beside the brooding horseman. The older man looked up at the frustrated figure.

'I thank you for undertaking this mission, Iron Eyes,' he said gratefully.

'The colonel threatened to have me hung,' the gaunt horseman said in a low dry whisper. 'Besides, that old galoot wants my horse, and I can't allow that. I only agreed to help you because of that, Smith.'

Although the words dismissed Iron Eyes' actions as being totally selfish, Smith sensed the opposite. He could tell that beneath his almost satanic appearance, Iron Eyes was far more human than most.

'I don't believe a word of it, son,' he said.

Iron Eyes looked at the small man who had been weathered by this harsh climate and nodded.

'Believe what you like,' he rasped.

Smith squinted up at the man he knew had more

chance of achieving this perilous mission successfully than any other living soul.

'I know these parts better than most, Iron Eyes,' he stated as his companion pulled out a dry twisted tobacco stick from his inside pocket and rammed it into his mouth. 'I've lived in this damn forest for the better part of my life. Together we have hope on our side. We'll find my girls.'

Thoughtfully, Iron Eyes chewed on the cigar as he looked through the darkness at the settler. Even the blackness of the forest could not conceal the pain in Smith's face from the bounty hunter's eyes.

'You know where Red Feather's camp is?' he asked as he continued to chew the cigar as his long fingers searched for a dry match.

Smith shook his head. 'Nope. I didn't even know that the Sioux had come this far into the forest. Most of the Injuns I've bumped into over the years have been Cree or Cheyenne. They never troubled me. I didn't even know that the Sioux were in this damn forest.'

'Strange for them to be this far away from the Dakotas, Smith,' Iron Eyes said. 'They seldom stray from their hunting grounds.'

Smith leaned closer to his tall companion as the bounty hunter reached back and opened one of the saddle-bag satchels and pulled out a bottle of whiskey. He was surprised that the infamous hunter of wanted men seemed to know nothing of what was happening in what was known as the Wild West.

'Ain't you heard about the Injun wars, boy?' the

old-timer questioned the bounty hunter. 'They reckon that thousands of white men have entered the Dakotas looking for gold in the Black Hills.'

'That's Sioux territory, ain't it?' Iron Eyes asked as he extracted the cork and took a swig. 'I thought the government gave that land to them.'

'They did, but those gold hunters are being escorted into the Black Hills by the military anyway,' Smith shrugged. 'The Sioux have been virtually driven up here by the cavalry. A lot of tribes are pretty angry about that. That's the reason they built Fort Liberty.'

Thoughtfully, Iron Eyes pushed the cork back into the neck of the bottle and returned it to his saddle-bags.

'That explains a lot,' he hissed. 'So that's why them Injuns are so darn ornery. I thought it was just me they didn't like, but now I'm starting to see things a lot clearer.'

'It ain't just you they've been shooting at, son,' Smith explained. 'They attacked a heavily armed platoon of troopers a while back. Killed most of them.'

'That ain't healthy,' Iron Eyes sighed as the fumes of the whiskey burned its way down into his guts. 'That means that they've got rifles and ammunition. Injuns are dangerous enough without them getting their hands on guns.'

'Right enough,' Smith agreed.

Suddenly the voice of Poke Spencer piped up behind Smith and Iron Eyes as he angrily snarled at

119

the two men. The noisy storm made it impossible for the five souls behind the settler and the bounty hunter to hear what they were discussing. That was making Spencer anxious.

'What you *hombres* talking about?' Spencer growled. 'You planning something? I don't like being kept in the dark when I'm risking my life just being here.'

'Shut up,' Captain Baker snarled at the prisoner.

'You can't give me orders out here, Baker,' Spencer snapped back at the officer. 'We've got a right to know if that damn scarecrow is planning something which might shorten our lives, ain't we?'

Tolley moved his horse forward and rammed the barrel of his rifle into Spencer's side. Even the darkness could not hide the fury in the winded prisoner.

'You heard the captain, Spencer,' Tolley said. 'Shut the hell up or I'll execute you right here. Savvy?'

Spencer's eyes darted between the six riders who surrounded him and then snorted.

'I savvy, Sergeant,' he begrudgingly grunted. 'Just remember that you varmints might need our help when we bump into them hostiles.'

Iron Eyes had sat watching the ruckus silently and then returned his attention to the old man seated beside him.

He cleared his throat.

'I need you to guide us to your cabin, Smith,' he said dryly as he steadied the horse beneath him.

Smith was confused. 'But I figured you'd want to try and find Red Feather's camp, Iron Eyes. How come you want to head to my old cabin? My daughters are long gone from there.'

'I know they are, but there could be some clues there which might tell me which way they went,' the bounty hunter explained as he glanced back at the horsemen behind them. 'I'm a tracker but I need something to track.'

Smith sorrowfully shook his head.

'It's been too long since my girls were abducted, sonny,' he sighed with a heavy heart. 'All the tracks would have been washed away by now.'

Iron Eyes finally located a dry match and scratched it across the horn of his saddle and then brought its flickering flame up to the end of the cigar. He filled his lungs with smoke and then tossed the match at the wet ground.

'Even Injuns leave tracks that I can follow, Smith,' he said with a satisfied smile etched into his shadowy features. As the last of the smoke escaped through his teeth he raised his arm and indicated for the troopers to follow.

'They do?' Smith asked as he gathered up his long reins.

Iron Eyes tapped his spurs.

'They sure do, old-timer,' he said, the smoke hanging around his wide shoulders. 'Nobody can ride through a forest as dense as this one without leaving clues to those who can read them. I can read them as clear as most folks can read books.'

The seven horsemen started to ride deeper into the forest with the gaunt bounty hunter at their head. Flashes of lightning momentarily illuminated the

121

dense terrain as the storm outside the forest grew even angrier.

'This is perfect weather for what I've got planned,' he said as his mount moved through the undergrowth and trees.

Smith tapped his spurs into the flanks of his own horse and stayed close to the hideous figure. The elderly settler knew that whatever the creature known as Iron Eyes had planned, it was going to be bloody.

Bloodier than anything any of them had ever experienced.

FOURTEEN

The seven horsemen drove their mounts through the dense woodland towards the hidden cabin which had been the home of Henry Smith and his daughters. Only Smith himself knew the way to the remote wooden structure set in the heart of the forest. The elderly settler rode at the head of the small troop of men and horses and expertly guided them ever deeper into the trees.

Iron Eyes remained just behind the elderly Smith as the seasoned settler guided them up a steep slope until they reached a small clearing. The storm was still raging above the tree tops, and during a flash of brilliant lightning the seven men spotted the crude but solid cabin on the other side of the cleared ground.

The men were about to dismount when Iron Eyes raised his hand and swung around on his saddle. Even the rain could not hide his serious expression from the six others.

'You men stay glued to them saddles,' he drawled deeply.

Silently the bounty hunter swung his long left leg

over the head of his horse and slid to the ground. The sound of the driving rain muffled the thud his mule-eared boots made as they hit the ground. He gave his horse's reins to Smith, then moved cautiously across the open ground towards the small cabin. Iron Eyes was like a panther as he navigated a route to the side of the structure and pressed his back against it. His keen eyesight darted all around the area before he edged round the corner and then entered the abandoned home.

He moved to the upturned table and plucked an oil lamp off the floor. A gentle shake of it beside his ear informed the bounty hunter that there were a few drops of coal-tar oil left in its reservoir. As the gaunt figure placed the lamp on top of the stone fireplace his thumbnail scratched a match and touched the lamp's wick; it lit up the room as Iron Eyes turned its brass wheel.

Iron Eyes could hear his six companions ride across the sodden clearing towards the cabin as he studied the interior for clues. It was no surprise to the experienced hunter that there seemed to be little evidence of the abduction.

Then as the six horsemen drew up outside the cabin, Iron Eyes noticed a small amulet on the wooden floor. The tall bounty hunter stooped and plucked up the silver trinket and held it close to his face; he studied the amulet carefully.

As the others crowded around the open doorway, Iron Eyes looked up at them. He held the silver object in his hand and clenched his fist around it as he forced his way through the men towards his mount. He opened the closest flap of his saddle-bags and pulled out one of the bottles as he considered his find thoughtfully.

Smith moved back into the rain and stared at the tall man carefully. He alone sensed that Iron Eyes had found something inside his cabin.

'What you got there?' he asked as he pointed at the bounty hunter's fist.

Iron Eyes looked up at the seasoned old man and then showed the silver object to Smith. 'I found this.'

Smith took hold of the silver item and then looked into the bullet-coloured eyes that sparkled in the lamp light.

'What is it?' Smith asked. 'It don't look like anything I've ever seen before.'

'It's a trophy,' said Iron Eyes as he pulled the cork from the whiskey bottle and took a long swallow. With the fiery liquid burning a path into his stomach, he moved closer to the confused Smith. 'I've seen them before. They usually wrap around the arm. This is a decoration fixed to a main piece.'

'I don't understand, Iron Eyes.'

'These are only worn by the sons of the chief, Smith,' Iron Eyes explained as he quickly downed a quarter of the bottle's contents. 'And only the Sioux tend to adorn themselves with such fancy jewellery. That means one of your gals put up a pretty good fight and tore this off the arm of Red Feather.'

'Just like I figured,' Smith said angrily.

Iron Eyes gave a nod of his head. His long hair

whipped the air as the bounty hunter glared through the rain at the five men sheltering inside the cabin. They seemed to think they were going to sit out the storm in the cabin. They were wrong. Totally wrong.

Iron Eyes intended to use the foul weather to their advantage, and refused to allow the driving rain to dampen his resolve. The bounty hunter knew that the Indian camp would be far easier to locate in the vast forest while the storm continued. Men of all colours and creeds use fire to warm their bones against the elements. But fires make smoke, and smoke is like a magnet to a skilled hunter. Iron Eyes pushed the cork back into the bottle neck and returned it to his saddlebags.

His piercing stare caught the attention of Baker and Tolley before the prisoners noticed. Iron Eyes gestured impatiently with his arm.

'C'mon,' he growled threateningly. 'We've got a long ride before we track down them gals and the bastards who are holding them against their will.'

Poke Spencer moved to the doorway and stared through the rainfall at the emaciated bounty hunter. He clenched a fist and shook it at the tall bedraggled figure before them.

'Are you loco?' Spencer yelled. 'I'm for building a fire in this cabin and us drying ourselves out before we do any more riding. I'm damn tired of you giving us orders and surely I'll kill you if you keep doing it.'

Both Kelly and Peters grunted in agreement with the oldest of the convicted prisoners. Tolley and

Baker stood behind the three with their weapons drawn.

Iron Eyes looked hard at them.

There was no hint of any emotion in his brutalized features as he slowly turned to face the loud-spoken Spencer. He pointed at the horses and then glared through narrowed eyes at them again.

'Get mounted before I kill you, Spencer,' he snarled through his scarred lips. 'You might be armed, but it's a long time since you handled a six-shooter. You're sadly out of practice.'

Spencer edged forward. 'When did you last kill someone?'

'Yesterday,' Iron Eyes answered truthfully. 'I gutted an Injun with my knife. Damned if I didn't enjoy it. To tell the truth I'm ready to do it again.'

'You done what?' Spencer nearly choked on his words as he realized that the notorious bounty hunter was deadly serious.

'Maybe you need a demonstration,' Iron Eyes hissed like a lethal sidewinder ready to strike out at it next victim. 'Maybe I oughta show you.'

FIFTEEN

Kelly and Peters looked at the open-mouthed face of Spencer and then backed away from him. Then they watched as Iron Eyes strode toward the shaking Spencer and stared down into his face. The gruesome bounty hunter clenched his left hand and violently punched the startled Spencer with his bony fist. The prisoner's head flew sideways as the impact of the sudden blow found its target. Before Spencer had time to react, Iron Eyes brought his clenched fist back across his jaw. Spencer's head was thrown back in the opposite direction.

Dazed by the powerful punches, all Spencer could do was rock on his boots as his fellow convicts held him upright with outstretched hands. But Iron Eyes wasn't finished. As the lamplight danced across his savagely maimed face he loomed over Spencer and watched the blood trail from the corners of his mouth. The tall killer stared with unblinking eyes down at the stunned man before him and gritted his teeth. Iron Eyes' mutilated features resembled something from Hell as he silently watched the fear grow in the man before him.

Spencer had not seen the face so clearly before this moment and was terrified by the sight. The flickering amber lamplight displayed every scar of Iron Eyes' nightmarish countenance, and justified the tall tales of his being the spawn of Satan himself. Poke Spencer started to shake.

He wanted to run and shield his eyes from the sight before him, but all he could do was shake uncontrollably. He tried to speak, but no words came from his open mouth. It was as though an unseen noose was throttling his throat. Then suddenly Iron Eyes grabbed Spencer's collar with one hand as his other bony hand produced his blood-stained Bowie knife. As the cold steel pressed into the flesh of Spencer's throat a wry grin etched the bounty hunter's hideous face.

For a few seemingly endless moments, every other member of the small troop thought that the humourless Iron Eyes was going to dispatch the convicted killer. Both Baker and Tolley glanced at one another but did not know what they should do. There was nothing in army regulations that came remotely close to this, so they remained silent. Iron Eyes pressed his face into the wide-eyed Spencer's and growled like a ferocious wild animal.

'Do you feel lucky, Spencer?' he whispered at a pitch only the frightened man could hear. 'Do you reckon you can do what hundreds of folks ain't been able to do?'

Spencer again vainly attempted to speak but only

blood left his mouth as he felt the knife's honed blade scrape chunks of beard off his face.

Iron Eyes released his grip and pushed the startled man into the arms of his cohorts. His icy stare burned into the three men dismissively.

'Never rile me up again, Spencer,' Iron Eyes warned the terrified prisoner. He then backed away from the cabin and returned his knife to the neck of his boot. 'Now get your backsides on them horses.'

Even though the Indians had long departed the abandoned cabin, the tracking skills of the deadly bounty hunter could not be outdone. His honed instincts had mercilessly tracked down and dispatched countless wanted outlaws over the years, and as far as Iron Eyes was concerned this was no different. Tracking was tracking. Whether it was a rabbit, a murderous bandit or an untold number of Indian warriors, if they left marks on the ground, Iron Eyes would find them.

The pitifully lean bounty hunter held the saddle horn and poked his boot into the stirrup, then mounted the horse in one swift action and steered the animal away from the cabin. The six men walked back out into the pouring rain and mounted their sodden horses. Most of them doubted the horrific bounty hunter's ability to find the Indian camp and the two young hostages. Only Henry Smith sensed that the brooding Iron Eyes could achieve the seemingly impossible.

They swung their horses around and watched the skeletal horseman moving his mount around the wet ground until he spotted something that alerted his keen senses. Iron Eyes sat upright and signalled to the men to follow him.

That was what they did.

Blinding flashes of lightning lit up the clearing, then deafening thunderclaps shook the very ground itself. Yet the horsemen ignored the elements and followed the scarecrow as he urged them on with a long thin arm.

Iron Eyes slowly led the small troop away from the cabin and back into the depths of the forest. His unblinking eyes studied every broken twig and branch hanging from bushes and tree trunks and enabled him to expertly calculate the route the Indians had taken after capturing Beth and Loretta Smith.

He was like a hound with the scent of its prey in his nostrils as he urged the cavalry horse on into the unkindly forest. Even the unholy darkness could not hide the tell-tale signs from his icy stare as Iron Eyes forged ever onward through the most difficult of terrains.

Few ordinary men would have reasoned the strange winding route the warring natives had taken, but Iron Eyes was far from ordinary. He alone knew how animals and men alike travel through uncharted regions to avoid being trailed. Iron Eyes kept hitting the shoulders of his mount with the ends of his reins to keep it travelling at an ever increasing pace, as if it were imperative not to lose a moment. He knew that they were probably riding to their collective deaths, but that did not matter to the bounty hunter. He had vowed to himself to rescue the girls and get them safely back to Fort Liberty, and that was what he intended to do.

As excitement swelled inside him, Iron Eyes kept driving his spurs into the bloody flanks of his mount as he caught the scent of campfire smoke in his flared nostrils. This was the thrill of the hunt, and it never failed to get his juices boiling to a feverish pitch.

As the mysterious horseman led the pack of riders who desperately tried to keep up with him, he resembled something more akin to another infamous creature of the night. His long mane of black hair beat up and down on his trail coat and resembled the wings of a bat in search of sanctuary.

The six riders behind him could not believe how Iron Eyes forced his mount on through every known obstacle without any thought for his own safety. They chased the haunting figure as he forced his way through the entangled undergrowth without slowing his pace. Iron Eyes was like a man possessed as he sensed that they were getting close to their goal.

None of the six riders behind the determined Iron Eyes could understand why the skeletal horseman seemed to be increasing his horse's speed with every thrust of his spurs. They could not fathom how Iron Eyes was able to withstand the razor-sharp bramble vines and keep moving ever onwards. It was as if he were immune to the pain that the thorns inflicted when they ripped at his flesh.

Silently, Captain Baker looked at Tolley and shrugged. The sergeant nodded in agreement to the unspoken amazement that they both felt as they watched the bounty hunter repeatedly lash his long reins across his mount's shoulders. All the six men could do was dutifully follow.

Then as Iron Eyes reached a break in the trees he pulled back sharply on his reins and held his mount in check as he waited for the others to catch up with him. Both horse and its rider were bleeding from the countless cuts and grazes they had endured on the painful ride to this spot.

Iron Eyes pulled a long cigar from his coat pocket and pushed it between his teeth as the six horsemen caught up and stopped their own horses on each side of his own. The bounty hunter said nothing as he continued to stare ahead of them into the wall of trees. His long digits extracted a match from his inside pocket while the others steadied their exhausted horses. Iron Eyes struck the match with his thumbnail, then swiftly cupped its flame and sucked in smoke. When his lungs were filled with the strong smoke he tossed the spent match aside.

'Why'd you stop, Iron Eyes?' Spencer growled, the hate evident in his voice.

Iron Eyes did not reply, but sucked on the flavoursome cigar for a few moments before handing the weed to Smith. The old man enjoyed the unfamiliar taste of the smoke as Iron Eyes leaned back and pulled the half empty bottle of whiskey from his saddle-bags. He pulled its cork with his sharp teeth and spat it at the bushes.

There was an unfamiliar air about the gaunt horseman as his bony fingers gripped the whiskey bottle and sat motionless on the cavalry mount. He had faced overwhelming odds many times, but this was different. His mind raced back to the memory of another female that he had chosen to rescue. His eyes strayed to the aged settler who sat close to him. Henry Smith was confident that the mysterious Iron Eyes would save his daughters from a fate that none of them had spoken of. But Iron Eyes was not so sure that either of the girls was still alive.

He turned his attention to the others. The convicts were dangerous but had yet to prove that they were a match for Red Feather or his fellow warriors. Soon they would be tested, but the gaunt bounty hunter had little faith in their abilities. He had encountered many of their breed and had found them all lacking in the one thing vital in the wilds: they lacked courage.

Captain Baker was a young officer. This was his first commission since graduating from military school. It was yet to be seen if the youngster could stand up to the test when the shooting started.

Only Leo Tolley could be relied upon to fight. He had fought shoulder to shoulder alongside Colonel Jay during the brutal civil war. Iron Eyes could not imagine what atrocities he had been part of, but he knew that even to have survived those battles meant that he was tough.

The horseman glanced heavenwards. The storm was still at fever pitch above them. Occasionally shafts of light splintered through the tree canopies and lit up the surrounding area.

Iron Eyes took a long swallow of the powerful liquor and then rested the bottle on the saddle-horn as he stared ahead into the trees.

'Why did you stop, Iron Eyes?' Baker asked as he carefully moved his horse to the side of his strange companion. 'You were forcing your horse through those bushes back there at an insane pace. Now you've stopped. Why?'

'Answer the captain, Iron Eyes,' Kelly snarled.

Iron Eyes lifted the bottle to his lips and then took another long swallow. The fumes cleared his head as he handed the bottle to the cavalry officer.

'Have yourself a drink, Captain,' the bounty hunter instructed the officer. 'It'll burn the damp out of you.'

Baker took a swig from the bottle and shuddered as the whiskey carved a trail into his belly. He then passed the whiskey bottle to Poke Spencer.

'Share this rotgut, Spencer,' Baker said.

The bottle was passed between the three convicted men. They each started to feel the effects of the fiery liquor as it warmed their bones. Then Tolley sniffed at the air and caught a scent he hadn't noticed before. It was not the aroma of the cigar that Smith was happily puffing on, but it was smoke.

'Can you boys smell that smoke yonder?' he asked his fellow travellers as he shared the whiskey with them. 'Can you?'

Baker was quick to sniff at the damp air and then began to nod at the sergeant. 'You're right, Sergeant. That's campfire smoke.'

Every eye turned to the bounty hunter. Now they

each knew exactly why Iron Eyes had stopped his exhausted mount. A cold shudder ran through each and every one of them.

Iron Eyes reached back and hauled another whiskey bottle from the saddle-bags and extracted its cork. He took a long swallow and sighed heavily.

'I wondered when you varmints would notice the smoke,' he said as he squinted through the long strands of limp hair that dangled before his deathly stare. 'I smelled it a half mile back. That's why I quickened my pace.'

Baker's expression suddenly altered.

'Do you mean we're close to the Indian camp?' he asked the skeletal man beside him.

'Yep,' The bounty hunter nodded. 'That's what it means.'

The six men who surrounded the wide-shouldered, expressionless Iron Eyes quickened the speed with which they drank the amber liquor as it suddenly dawned on them that the legendary tracker had done exactly as he had vowed he would do: he had led them right to the doorstep of the Sioux warriors.

After downing a third of his fresh bottle, Iron Eyes handed the remainder to the men, just as they had taken the first and drained it.

'Finish this for me,' he rasped. 'This ain't a job to tackle if you're sober, boys.'

The nervous men feverishly drank the whiskey, knowing that it might be the last time any of them would taste anything but blood in their mouths. Only when the bottle was emptied did the lean horseman dismount and secure his reins to a branch. Iron Eyes turned and glared through the gloom at them as Peters tossed the second bottle aside.

'By my reckoning we've got three hours before sunrise,' he said through gritted teeth. 'That's how long we've got to rescue them gals and get back here.'

Baker dropped from his horse and tied his long reins to a tree as the others slowly followed suit. The officer moved to the ghostly figure and looked straight at Iron Eyes.

'We're walking to their camp?' he asked.

Iron Eyes gave a nod of his head.

SIXTEEN

Iron Eyes moved silently through the dense under-growth with his six followers close on his heels. The light from the temporary encampment grew brighter as the honed instincts of the notorious bounty hunter drew him ever closer to his prey.

For the first time in many a long while, Iron Eyes was doing what he had grown used to doing when he was a youth. He was advancing without fear, towards men who would kill him without a second thought. In all his life he had never encountered any tribe of the natives who had once reigned supreme in the Americas, who did not try to kill him on sight.

The large fire in the heart of the encirclement of tepees still crackled and spat its warmth at the handful of Indians who were awake. A small number of squaws went about their nightly duties as most of their menfolk slept in the tepees.

The keen eyes of the bounty hunter darted around the area and spotted several warriors who might put a stop to them locating the Smith sisters: it was obvious to Iron Eyes that these few warriors were acting as sentries.

A thick cloud billowed up from the large fire as logs blackened and crumbled to ash in the heart of the fiery centre of the flames. Iron Eyes dropped on to one knee and stared through the entangled bushes at the women who continually fed the flames with kindling.

Henry Smith crawled to the side of the tall figure. Iron Eyes looked to the five other men who were to their right and made them all drop to their knees and bellies with a swift hand gesture.

'How many of them do you think there are, sonny?' Smith asked his companion as every scar on his unholy face was illuminated by the light of the flames.

'I can only guess, old-timer,' he whispered. 'I've spotted three warriors wide awake and wandering around the boundaries of the camp, and there are five fully erected tepees which can hold up to ten folks.'

Smith looked troubled, reasoning there could be as many as fifty Indians hidden inside the rawhide tents. He rubbed his bearded chin and started to tremble.

'There's too many of them, boy,' he reluctantly admitted.

Iron Eyes lowered his head. His long hair hung limply and covered his gruesome features as he slowly sucked in air through his flared nostrils. After a few silent moments he tilted his head and stared straight into the defeated expression of the old settler.

'There's never too many, Smith,' he rasped.

'How can you be so damn confident?' Smith asked

the infamous bounty hunter.

Iron Eyes continued to watch the females gathered around the campfire as they carefully worked. His eyes then strayed to the only tepee with its blanket flap left open. Females walked to and from the tent carrying baskets of ingredients for the pot.

'Most of them warriors are dead asleep at this time. The only menfolk I can see are real tuckered sentries. This all plays in our favour.' He hissed as a simple plan started to hatch inside his lethal mind. 'I got me a notion that might just work. Keep believing in me.'

A new look of hope filled Smith's face.

'Do you still reckon it's possible to save my gals?' he asked the unblinking horror beside him. 'Is there still a chance, boy? Is there?'

Iron Eyes gave a slow nod.

'Only dead critters ain't got any hope left. I've got it all straight in my head, I reckon them girls will soon be safe, old-timer,' he vowed before adding a foot-note. 'If shooting erupts down there you and the rest of these boys better start unleashing lead.'

Smith gulped and nodded.

Summoning every scrap of his merciless skills, Iron Eyes moved stealthily past Smith and vanished into the thick undergrowth. As the six men crouched a mere ten yards from the camp and watched the bounty hunter vanish from view, they suddenly felt very vulnerable.

Suddenly they realized they were alone.

SEVENTEEN

Fuelled by the powerful whiskey that still smouldered inside them, the men had followed Iron Eyes away from their cavalry mounts to a place where they could almost reach out and touch the warring Indians. Now they were alone in the forest and the effects of the hard liquor were wearing off fast.

Captain Baker raised the barrel of his rifle and cocked its hammer as he trained it through the entangled bushes. The inexperienced officer looked to Spencer, Kelly and Peters and silently instructed them to follow suit. The convicts nervously eased the long barrels of their weapons through gaps in the bushes and trained them on the blazing campfire.

Only Sergeant Tolley remained calm behind the four men holding their rifles in readiness. The seasoned soldier knelt a few feet behind the four others and simply watched and waited. This was not the first time he had been so close to a potential enemy and although nervous, he remained level-headed.

Smith lay on his belly and kept watching the Indian

womenfolk as they continued to go about their nightly duties. He clutched the rifle to his chest and simply stared through the tangle of brush. His mind kept shifting between curiosity as to what Iron Eyes was doing, to hopes that he might glimpse his daughters in the camp.

Iron Eyes carefully negotiated a route through the brush which took him around the circled tepees. He used the honed blade of his Bowie knife to silently cut every vine from his path. Few men would have had either the courage or ability to move so confidently around the tall tepees as Iron Eyes searched for the unseen Smith sisters. The horrifically maimed bounty hunter knew that if any of the warring braves caught sight of him, they would instantly turn their wrath upon him.

He had already passed their colourful ponies hidden a few yards behind the tepees and made a mental note of how many of them there were. Some confiscated cavalry horses were among the Indians resting mounts.

Iron Eyes' thin frame came to an abrupt halt as he reached the last tepee. He quickly crouched as he heard the heavy footsteps of one of the Sioux sentries pacing a few feet ahead of him. His hand gripped the bone handle of his knife even tighter as his eyes stared through the limp strands of his long hair at the approaching brave. Iron Eyes remained perfectly still and watched the Indian as he paused between two of the tepees.

The warrior had a buffalo fur robe hanging on his

shoulders as a protection against the cool night breeze. The bounty hunter could tell that the muscular Sioux warrior was tired and close to falling asleep. 'I'll help you sleep,' he vowed in an almost undetectable drawl. 'I'll help you sleep permanently.' He slowly rose like a ghost from his position at the edge of the tall tent, and started to close the distance between himself and the unsuspecting guard.

Before the Indian knew what was happening, Iron Eyes grabbed him around the head and mouth. His thumb and fingers smothered any potential cry for help. Then the lean bounty hunter pushed his boot into the back of the Indian's knee and pulled him backwards. The knife blade slid through the buffalo robe into the flesh of the stunned Sioux brave. A muffled gasp filtered between the bounty hunter's bony fingers as Iron Eyes eased the limp body down to the ground.

There was no sign of emotion in Iron Eyes' haunted features as he dispatched the Indian to the afterlife. He looked up and stared between the tepees at the females close to the massive campfire as they continued to toil.

They had not heard anything, he reasoned.

Within a mere heartbeat, Iron Eyes had dragged the body into the bushes, thrown the fur robe over it and then returned to the spot where he had been before spying the dutiful sentry. A faint sound caught his honed hearing and drew his attention. His head turned on its scrawny neck and listened to every sound within the camp.

143

He instantly dismissed the snoring which emanated from the majority of the tepees and concentrated on one of the tepees closest to him. Iron Eyes made his way as fast as he could to where he had determined the sounds were coming from.

Iron Eyes crouched down, straining to hear where the noises were coming from – then he carefully moved to the next tepee. Female voices came from inside the large tent beside him. His bowed head pressed against the rawhide and listened as hard as he could. Although he could not understand what was being said he knew that it was definitely women talking. One spoke in the native tongue, but two of the voices were speaking English. The long bony fingers of his left hand pushed the sweat-soaked hair off his face as he forced his long lean frame into the shadows.

His eyes tightened as they focused on the females who were still busy around the camp fire. The scent of the meal they were preparing filled his nostrils.

He rubbed the drool from the corners of his mouth as a shadow flashed across his kneeling form. Iron Eyes gripped the deadly Bowie knife tightly, and slowly drew himself up to his full height and watched another of the Indian sentries moving uncomfortably close to where he was standing in the shadow of the tepee. The Indian was obviously looking for the man that Iron Eyes had just sent to the happy hunting ground and left hidden beneath his buffalo robe in the brush.

Tension gripped his craw even more tightly than he

144

was gripping the knife handle. Iron Eyes knew that if the Indian were to find the body he would instantly alert the rest of the encampment that they had an uninvited intruder in their midst.

Like a living phantom, Iron Eyes took a backward step and vanished from sight in the dense forest. Although he was only feet away from the tepee that he now knew held the Smith sisters, he could not be seen by even the least observant of eyes.

The Indian guard was becoming more and more anxious as he vainly searched for his fellow sentry. Iron Eyes watched the Indian carefully as he started to check behind the tepees. Iron Eyes then realized that the inquisitive warrior was getting close to where he had left the dead Indian.

Too damn close.

Living up to his reputation of being a living ghost, the tall figure slid silently through the undergrowth to where the Indian was searching for his companion. His ghostly figure stood only two feet from the increasingly troubled Indian, yet remained totally invisible behind the foliage.

The warrior's feet suddenly felt the fur robe beneath his moccasins. He looked down and started to investigate further, cautiously stooping over and reaching out his hands to remove the buffalo skin.

As the Sioux warrior took hold of the large robe, two arms flew out from the black bushes. Before the Indian knew what was happening, the bony hands had grabbed his head and violently twisted it around. The sound of snapping bones filled the damp air as the bounty hunter made sure of his kill.

The warrior slumped over the body at his feet. Iron Eyes quickly drew out his knife again and thrust it mercilessly into the chest of the warrior. A sickening gasp came from the stricken Indian as Iron Eyes repeated the action.

The bounty hunter poked the blade back into the neck of his mule-eared boot and released his hold on the stricken Indian. As the body fell to the ground, Iron Eyes used his foot to push the lifeless body into the bushes. He stepped over the corpse and then made his way back as quickly as he could to where he had detected the female voices.

Iron Eyes stopped beside the expertly stitched walls of the tall tent, and glimpsed across the small clearing between himself and the fire. He immediately noticed that there were now four squaws around the fire, and they were all Indians.

Taking a gamble that the tepee was now only occupied by the Smith sisters, Iron Eyes stabbed the blade of his Bowie knife into the taut rawhide wall and dragged it down towards the ground. The gaunt bounty hunter knew that if he was wrong he would have every single Indian attacking him before he had time to rescue the young females.

Iron Eyes then slid the honed blade back into the neck of his boot and tore the rawhide wall apart to reveal the startled Beth and Loretta. Both girls were huddled together, in sudden fear of the shadowy form that poked its head into the tepee and gestured to them with an outstretched arm.

146

'C'mon, gals,' Iron Eyes feverishly urged the Smith sisters.

They immediately responded to the bounty hunter and hastily got to their feet: they ran to this man shielded by darkness and clambered though the crude hole.

'Follow me,' whispered their saviour, with urgency in his low voice.

Faster than he had moved since embarking on his perilous mission, Iron Eyes turned on his heels and quickly led the girls around the back of the tepees. Neither Loretta nor Beth had any reason to know that their saviour had already killed two of their captors as they reached the last of the tepees. As Iron Eyes paused in the dark shadows the girls rested behind his wide back and awaited his signal to run. To run for their lives. Knowing that his appearance would probably terrify the girls, Iron Eyes deliberately kept his mutilated face turned away from them.

'When you get to a cleared trail that I've carved out,' he whispered through his mane of long hair, 'keep running. Your pa is at the end of it.'

The sisters could barely control their relief and excitement as the tall bounty hunter summoned up the dregs of his exhausted stamina. Iron Eyes pointed to where he had carved out their trail with his trusty Bowie knife.

'Run!' he hissed.

The girls were about to follow his instructions and bolt for the entangled bushes when suddenly a Sioux guard appeared from around the side of the tepee right in front of the emaciated bounty hunter.

Both men came to an abrupt halt as they gazed into one another's startled faces. The warrior dragged his tomahawk from his belt and swung at Iron Eyes. The edge of the axe caught the bounty hunter across his shoulder and knocked him off balance momentarily. Ignoring the pain that racked through his thin body, Iron Eyes threw himself at the Indian with all his might. They grappled feverishly across the damp ground as the females looked on helplessly.

Soon the Smith sisters would realize just how lethally dangerous Iron Eyes truly was.

EIGHTEEN

Both men separated and glared with deadly eyes. If looks alone could kill, then both Iron Eyes and the Indian would have died on the spot. But they were not dead yet. This Indian sentry was more alert than his deceased counterparts, and screamed out at the top of his voice before lungeing at the lean bounty hunter. The savage call echoed through the encampment and stirred even the heaviest of the sleeping warriors.

As the warrior pulled back his hand to repeat his action Iron Eyes kicked out and caught the wrist of the Indian. The tomahawk went flying up into the air but Iron Eyes realized that the warrior's guttural outcry had already alerted the majority of the Indians behind his broad shoulders. It was pointless for the bounty hunter to remain silent any longer. The damage had already been done.

Iron Eyes could already hear the sound of awaking Indians, and swiftly pulled one of his Navy Colts from his deep trail-coat pockets, cocked its hammer and fired.

The sound was deafening as a plume of lead venom spewed from its long barrel and carved a fiery lightning bolt at the Sioux warrior standing between them and the relative safety of the dark forest. The Indian took the full power of the blast as the bullet punched a hole through his middle. He buckled and fell at the feet of his emotionless executioner.

Iron Eyes turned and looked at the terrified females behind his coat tails.

'Hitch up them dresses,' he ordered. 'We got us some running to do.'

The girls did not need telling twice, and ran after the man with the smoking six-gun in his hand as Iron Eyes retraced his tracks between the trees and along the narrow path he had hacked through the undergrowth. Suddenly the air was filled with rifle fire as the Indians started to unleash the venom of their newly acquired weaponry at the fleeing figures.

'I hate Injuns,' he snarled as a volley of bullets flew all around them like a swarm of crazed hornets – 'I hate them worse than I hate cowboys.'

The bounty hunter returned fire as arrows joined the bullets and hurtled in his direction. It sounded like drums being beaten as the feathered projectiles embedded into the trees which surrounded him.

Then to Iron Eyes' relief, his six fellow rescuers started to fire their rifles from the ridge. The tranquillity was shattered as bullets traced through the darkness in both directions. Gunsmoke filled the confines of the forest quickly and drifted like phantoms above a graveyard.

With his free hand Iron Eyes grabbed the crouching sisters in turn, and pushed them ahead of him as he continued to fire his six-shooter at the irate Indians.

'Duck and run,' he commanded the pair. 'Keep moving before we're all as dead as that Injun I just killed.'

The chilling words hastened their pace.

The sight of the six men blasting their rifles down at the Indian camp was something which had to be seen to be believed. The girls fell on to their knees and hugged their tearful father as Iron Eyes stepped over them and moved close to Baker.

'You took your time before you opened up with them carbines, Baker,' Iron Eyes growled as he shook the smoking casings from his gun and speedily reloaded. 'What was you doing? Knitting me a tombstone?'

Captain Baker and the others were blasting their repeating rifles down the slope at the irate Indians. The sound of the deafening rifle fire muffled the sarcastic words from his ears.

'What happened?' the captain asked the gaunt figure who knelt down beside him. 'How come the Indians suddenly erupted like that?'

Iron Eyes finished pushing fresh bullets into his smoking chambers and tilted his head. 'Hell. I nearly got them gals out of there without firing a shot when I bumped into one hell of a noisy Injun, Captain. He bellowed so loud I reckon he woke up his ancestors.'

'Did you have to kill any of them?' Tolley asked as

he started pushed fresh ammunition into his exhausted rifle.

'Three of them,' Iron Eyes explained as he stared through the gunsmoke at the Injuns below their vantage point. 'I gutted two of the varmints and shot the last one. We would have gotten clean away if that last Injun hadn't screamed so damn loud.'

'How many of them are there?' Baker asked as suddenly an arrow came hurtling through the smoke and caught Kelly in the throat. The officer gritted his teeth and looked back at the bounty hunter who rested beside him. 'Could you tell how many Indians Red Feather has with him down there?'

Iron Eyes narrowed his eyes.

'There were four females down there, besides the Smith gals,' he started. 'Then there were a total of eighteen ponies and a few horses with army brands on their rumps hidden in the trees. I reckon that there were at least eighteen warriors besides them females before the shooting started. Squaws don't ride, they walk.'

Baker nodded. He was no wiser even after Iron Eyes had explained his crude reckoning to the officer.

A sickening scream behind the cavalry officer drew the bounty hunters' attention.

With blood pouring from his breast, Peters fell forward and then slid into the muddy ground. Spencer stared at his fellow convict as he forced fresh bullets into his rifles magazine. The last surviving member of the convicts turned Peters body over and stared in disbelief at the neat bullet hole in his chest.

'This ain't healthy, Baker,' Spencer shouted at the officer. 'We're getting picked off by them red devils one by one. We gotta run and get out of here.'

Iron Eyes looked over the captain's back at the terrified Spencer and shook his head. His cruel expression said more than words could ever convey.

'Try and kill some of them Injuns before they kill the rest of us, Spencer,' he said bluntly.

Poke Spencer suddenly rose up on his knees and levelled his rifle at the bounty hunter. His thumb cocked its hammer as a wicked grin etched his face.

'I'm through taking orders from a damn scarecrow,' he snarled at Iron Eyes. 'You're through ordering me about. I'm leaving you all to. . . .'

Poke Spencer did not finish his sentence. He would never finish anything ever again. The arrow in his chest would ensure that simple fact. The rifle became heavy in the hands of a dead man and slowly lowered to the ground as Spencer fell on to his side.

'Damn,' Iron Eyes disappointedly grunted. 'I was just about to blast his head off his shoulders.'

A frantic volley of bullets and arrows tore through the ridge where the surviving members of the Fort Liberty rescue team remained huddled.

Iron Eyes turned away from the sight of the dead bodies and looked at Tolley. He leaned close to the trooper and whispered in his ear.

'Get Smith and them gals away from here, Tolley,' he instructed the cavalryman. 'Get them to the horses and ride back to Fort Liberty with them.'

'I can't leave you and the captain,' Tolley objected.

'You might need my help.'

'Smith and his daughters need your help more than we do,' Iron Eyes insisted. 'You're the only one who knows how to use your weapons. If they bump into any stray Injuns, they'll not stand a chance without you.'

Reluctantly, the sergeant nodded and gathered the Smith family together before leading them away from the lean bounty hunter and the inexperienced cavalry officer into the surrounding forest.

'How many of them Indians do you figure are still alive, Iron Eyes?' Baker asked his companion as he gathered the dead men's rifles together.

Iron Eyes did not reply until there was a gap in the gunsmoke which gave him an uninterrupted view of the temporary encampment. His cruel eyes focused on the numerous dead bodies that were laid out around the campfire. The bounty hunter pushed a cigar between his teeth and struck a match. As the flame died down he brought it up to the end of his cigar and filled his lungs with smoke.

'Not too many by my figuring, Captain,' he said through a line of smoke. 'Looks like you boys are better shots than I gave you credit for.'

Baker got up on his knees and pushed his torso against a tree trunk and quickly counted the bodies before sliding back down next to the bounty hunter.

'I count sixteen Indians on the sand, Iron Eyes.' He stated firmly. 'That leaves about two if your reckoning was right.'

'At least two, Baker,' Iron Eyes tilted his head and pulled out his other Navy Colt from its resting place inside his deep coat pocket. 'I was only guessing that there were eighteen of the varmints.'

The face of George Baker suddenly went pale. His eyes widened as he stared in horror over the head of the bounty hunter at something behind the infamous bounty hunter. The young captain was frozen in terror. But at the same time Iron Eyes' keen hearing detected the sound of approaching moccasins, and without a moment's hesitation the scrawny bounty hunter rolled over to face the advancing Sioux warrior. Iron Eyes quickly raised both his guns and pulled back on his triggers.

The sound of two shots echoed around the area, and the bounty hunter watched as the rifle-toting Indian was knocked off his feet by the sheer impact of his well placed bullets. As the body landed in the mud, Iron Eyes rose to his feet and blasted his Navy Colts again.

Another Indian fell a few paces behind the first.

Iron Eyes was silent as he stared at both bodies in turn and then looked back at the trembling officer. He gave a grunt and then poked his smoking guns into his pants belt.

Baker scrambled to his feet as his eyes flashed between both warriors in turn. He gulped and moved closer to the bounty hunter and gave a nod of his head.

'How many of them are left, Iron Eyes?' he stammered.

Iron Eyes listened to the surrounding forest like a wolf listens in order to locate its prey. His haunting features then faced Baker.

'There ain't none of them left, Captain,' he replied dryly as he stepped over one of the lifeless Indians and walked to where the other had fallen.

Baker trailed the bounty hunter like a loyal hound dog to the Indian and stared through the shadows at the corpse with two perfectly placed bullet holes in its chest. He looked at Iron Eyes and hesitantly asked:

'What you looking at?'

Iron Eyes stepped over the body and started to walk through the brush as he started to follow the route that Tolley and the Smiths had taken. Baker hurried and caught up with the silent bounty hunter.

'What were you looking at back there?' he repeated.

'The second Injun,' Iron Eyes answered as he moved between the trees with the cavalry officer on his shoulder. 'I was just looking at the second of them Injuns.'

'But why, Iron Eyes?' Baker pressed as the two men walked through the forest. 'What was so interesting about him?'

Without missing a stride Iron Eyes replied:

'That was Red Feather,' he said.

With the sky suddenly getting lighter as a new day was about to be break, the cavalryman and the bounty hunter continued on silently to where they had left the horses.

FINALE

Trooper Jody Casson squinted over the high walls of the fortress and noticed the two horsemen as they guided their cavalry mounts back to the relative safety of Fort Liberty. The horsemen were travelling at a fast pace as if they wanted to put distance between themselves and the forest. Casson swung around and called down from the high parapet to draw the attention of those who were milling around within the parade ground.

'Two riders approaching,' the trooper cried out at the top of his voice. 'Looks like Captain Baker and that bounty hunter to me.'

Colonel Brice Jay looked out from his open office window and returned his pen to the inkwell. The seasoned officer rose up to his impressive height and adjusted his blue tunic before marching around his desk and retrieving his hat from the stand close to the open door.

Sergeant Tolley had already guided the Smith family safely back to Fort Liberty an hour earlier, and was dozing on the leather couch close to the open door.

Jay hesitated for a few moments and looked down

at his loyal friend who had willingly volunteered on the perilous mission against his superior's advice.

'Sleep, old friend,' Jay whispered gruffly before continuing out of the office at a brisk pace. 'You deserve a rest after what you've been through.'

The gates opened as Jay started to cross the parade ground.

The veteran officer stopped in his tracks as both Baker and Iron Eyes galloped into the fort and drew rein a matter of only a few feet away from Jay.

Baker dismounted and exchanged salutes with the smiling colonel. He then took hold of his lathered animal's long reins and led it towards the livery stables.

As the gates were secured again, Brice Jay studied the strange bounty hunter who glared through the hoof dust at him. There was a stony silence for a few moments as they just watched one another.

Then the devilishly maimed bounty hunter leaned back on the saddle and placed one of his twisted cigars between his scarred lips. As he struck a match and touched the end of the black tobacco stick he muttered in a low tone.

'I come back for my horse, Colonel,' he hissed through a cloud of smoke before dropping the spent match on to the sand. 'Just like I told you I would.'

Brice Jay sighed heavily as he watched the bounty hunter dismount and stride up to him. With the cigar gripped firmly by his teeth, Iron Eyes tilted his head and stared though his limp strands of hair and waited.

Colonel Jay was about to speak when he noticed the

wooden grips of the matched Navy Colts jutting out from behind the bounty hunter's belt buckle.

'Sergeant Tolley told me how you rescued those girls single-handed, Iron Eyes,' he said with the look of a gambler who had lost a hefty bet. 'I'm impressed.'

'I don't give a damn,' Iron Eyes growled as his bony hands hovered above the grips of his guns. 'I want my horse back. I told you what I'd do if you didn't return that stallion to me.'

'You did, didn't you?' Jay cleared his throat as he studied the unusual figure before him and noticed the bloodstains now covering his new trail coat. 'I think you're just loco enough to do it.'

'I want my horse, old man,' Iron Eyes repeated firmly. 'I killed me a lot of Injuns to rescue them gals. Now it's your turn to either honour your promise or make me kill you. I don't care which you choose.'

Jay gestured with his left arm. Iron Eyes glanced to where the colonel was indicating and saw the burly blacksmith leading the high-withered stallion towards them through the morning sunshine.

The bounty hunter returned his eyes to the colonel and gave a violent nod of his head. Then he took the reins from the liveryman and led the horse to the exhausted cavalry mount. Iron Eyes took the saddle-bags and tied them carefully behind the cantle of the ornate Mexican saddle. He then grabbed the silver horn of the saddle and hauled his aching body on to the back of the powerful horse.

'You're leaving?' Colonel Jay asked with genuine surprise in his voice as he watched the bounty hunter turn the palomino stallion to face the gates. 'I thought you'd rest up before tackling the long ride back to civilization.'

Iron Eyes signalled the pair of troopers to open the gates.

'I can't afford to stay here, Colonel,' he rasped as he removed the cigar from his lips and tapped its ash at the white sand. 'You might get another notion to part me from this old nag again.'

Brice Jay strode to the shoulder of the horse and looked up into the mutilated face of the strange bounty hunter. A wry smile filled his face.

'If I'd had twenty troopers like you ten years ago I'd have won the war in months, Iron Eyes,' he said.

Iron Eyes returned the cigar to his lips and filled his lungs with the strong smoke. As it lingered for a few moments in his emaciated body he glanced down at the colonel and shook his head.

'Maybe so – but who says I'd have been fighting on your side, old-timer?' he said before tapping his spurs into the flanks of the powerful horse and starting for the open gates. Once out of the gates Iron Eyes pulled the reins to his left and headed east. As the powerful stallion gathered pace, its master clung on to the horse's mane.

He had only one thought burning in his tortured mind: where was Squirrel Sally?